MW01126855

MURDER AND MOONSTONES

Crystal Cove Cozy Mysteries
Book One

By Cindy Stark

www.cindystark.com

Murder and Moonstones © 2019 C. Nielsen

Cover Design by Kelli Ann Morgan
Inspire Creative Services

All rights reserved

License Notes

This ebook is licensed for your personal enjoyment only. This ebook may not be re-sold or given away to other people. If you would like to share this book with another person, please purchase an additional copy for each recipient. If you're reading this book and did not purchase it, or it was not purchased for your use only, then please purchase your own copy. The ebook contained herein constitutes a copyrighted work and may not be reproduced, transmitted, downloaded, or stored in or introduced into an information storage and retrieval system in any form or by any means, whether electronic or mechanical, now known or hereinafter invented, without the express written permission of the copyright owner, except in the case of brief quotation embodied in critical articles and reviews. Thank you for respecting the hard work of this author.

This ebook is a work of fiction. The names, characters, places, and incidents are products of the writer's imagination or have been used fictitiously and are not to be construed as real. Any resemblance to persons, living or dead, actual events, locales or organizations is entirely coincidental.

MOONSTONE

A pearly white semiprecious stone.

A symbol for new beginnings.

The dreamy, ethereal stone channels the moon, a force that has the power to push and pull the tides of great oceans and human emotions.

Moonstone holds a nourishing, sensual, deeply feminine energy that knows how to heal and bring a person back to wholeness. It is the stone of the mother moon, deep healing waters, and sacred feminine energies.

Visit www.cindystark.com for more titles and release information. Sign up for Cindy's newsletter to ensure you're always hearing the latest happenings.

DISCLAIMER: All spells in this book are purely fictional and for fun.

CHAPTER ONE

Opal Mayland was close. So close.

Less than twenty minutes stood between her and Crystal Cove, Oregon, her childhood home. She'd spent the last several years in Sedona, Arizona, learning and practicing her craft.

She appreciated the teachers who'd worked with her on spells and potions, since that opportunity didn't exist for her in Crystal Cove, but she'd had enough of the desert heat. The lush green forests full of alders, spruce, and fir trees had called to her soul, and now she was finally back to the Oregon coast.

This morning, she'd woken super early so she could roll into town just past noon. Now, she was so close to home that she could taste the salt on the late springtime air that blew in through the car window.

Opal pressed harder on the accelerator, and the needle on the speedometer crept up. Her sparkly blue Mustang growled as its engine kicked in, and it eased into the next curve as smooth as the surface of a mountain lake.

She smiled, loving the thrill.

Rain speckled the windshield, and she turned on the wipers to whisk it away. She didn't mind. She loved the rain and salty ocean breezes more than just about anything in the world. She'd missed the Pacific Northwest's beauty almost as much as she'd missed her grandfather.

The urge to throw her arms around her grandpa, the town's police chief, was strong, and she hoped he wouldn't lecture her for coming home unannounced. She also hoped he'd learned to keep his share of crazy in check when it came to any kind of paranormal persons other than her. The fact that he'd accidentally married a witch never failed to give Opal a laugh.

The sight of a dark blue police SUV nestled amongst a cluster of trees along the side of the road reined in her thoughts. She flicked her gaze to the speedometer and cringed. Fourteen over the posted limit.

Red and blue lights flashed to life, and she groaned. She didn't need her grandfather to hear that the first thing she'd done on her first day back was to get a speeding ticket. He'd never let her live it down.

She let off the gas and weighed her chances of being able to talk the officer out of giving her a citation. She'd guess fifty-fifty, which wasn't great. But then another option popped into her mind.

What if she tried a redirection spell?

She'd been dying to try it out in the real world, but did she dare? If it worked, it would cause the officer to switch his focus to something else. If it didn't, then she might end up with a citation. So, really, what did she have to lose?

The loud chirp of the officer's siren brought her thoughts to the present and warned she was out of time.

She had to cast the spell now or never.

Do it, her inner voice said. *Do it.*

She glanced in the rearview mirror and released a steadying breath. "See that tree? See that ground? Stop your car and turn around. What you need is not me. Turn away, so mote it be."

The little buzz that she received from casting a successful spell heated her blood. Her mentors had warned not to use magic for selfish reasons too often, lest she invoke Karma to balance her efforts, but this one little thing shouldn't hurt.

She smiled and pressed the accelerator, expecting the officer would pull to the side of the road and then head in the opposite direction.

Seconds passed, and her nerves began to twitch. She continually flicked her gaze between the road ahead and her rearview mirror, but the officer wasn't stopping. In fact, he seemed closer than ever. The SUV's emergency lights remained bright, even with the increased spray of water her tires kicked up. Uncertainty tightened her throat, and she swallowed.

She'd try it again. Maybe she hadn't said something quite right.

"See that tree?" she whispered harsh and fast. "See that ground? Stop your car and turn around. What you need is not me. Turn away, so mote it be."

The officer turned on the siren full blast. It startled her so much that she thought her heart might stop beating.

Sweet mother of pearl.

Her spell hadn't worked, and now the officer was in hot pursuit after *her*. She'd become one of those idiot people her grandfather had told her about, the ones who thought they could somehow evade the law. She needed to pull over before the officer called for backup.

Her pulse thundered in her ears as she signaled, slowed, and came to a stop at the side of the road. The chance of talking her way out of a citation now had dropped significantly.

Then again, maybe she didn't need to worry so much. After all, she was home. As long as her grandfather hadn't switched out the entire police force, chances were good that she'd know the officer. Maybe she could plead for mercy and end up with only a strong lecture about speeding. This was manageable. Not the end of the world.

She exhaled and reined in her fears.

Spatters of rain on the windshield and the side mirror kept her from immediately identifying the tall, obviously male officer who approached. She lowered her window and cast her gaze downward in contrition, prepared to apologize.

"Step out of your car, ma'am."

The fierce authority in his voice surprised her, and she swung her gaze over her shoulder to see him better. The dark-haired officer with gorgeous green eyes placed his hand in warning on the butt of his gun.

Surprised, her breath caught in her throat, and she choked. "No, wait. You don't—"

"I *said*, step out of the car."

His voice was even and clear, and she had no doubt he meant what he said. Her brain emptied of all thoughts, and her hands flew into the air as though they had a mind of their own. The officer opened her door, and she awkwardly swiveled on her seat and stepped out into the light, misty rain.

The officer, perhaps a few years older than her, wore an official Crystal Cove Police Department jacket embroidered with his last name,

Keller. Short, midnight hair peeked from beneath his plastic-covered hat. But those intense green eyes intimidated her the most.

Officer Keller glanced beyond her and into the car as though searching for signs that she might be dangerous. "Name?"

She swallowed. "Opal Mayland."

His gaze pierced hers again. "Do you have a driver's license, Ms. Mayland?"

She nodded. "It's in the car. Should I get it?"

"Not until I tell you to."

He scrutinized every inch of her, leaving her feeling vulnerable and exposed. "Are you carrying any weapons, Ms. Mayland?"

Her negative response sounded more like a squeak.

He narrowed his eyes. "Why didn't you stop when I first flashed my lights?"

Oh dear. She widened her eyes into innocent ovals. "I did stop. That's why we're standing here in the rain."

Irritation sparked in his eyes, and she swore they darkened. He obviously did not appreciate her flippant response. "You did *eventually.* From my perspective, it appeared as though you'd attempted to outrun me first."

Her heart thundered in her chest, and she shook her head quickly. "No, sir. I...I panicked."

The white lie fell easily from her lips.

He lifted a brow, indicating he expected more from her in the way of an excuse.

She exhaled a nervous breath. "I know I should have stopped right away, but this crazy thought entered my mind, telling me I needed to hurry and get to a pull-off before I moved out of your way. So, I went faster. Then I realized that you were actually pulling *me* over, not chasing after someone else."

Even to her own ears, her lie sounded utterly ridiculous. She could only imagine what he must be thinking.

He stared, stone-faced. "You expect me to believe that."

Praying that he would do exactly that, she opened her hands, palms up and shrugged. "I have anxieties and don't always react in the most appropriate way."

She watched his face carefully, working hard to keep hers a mask of virtue. Instinctively, she reached out with her senses, trying to discover his hidden emotions but came back with nothing. Perhaps she should tell him who her grandfather was so that she could generate credibility, but her heart warned against it.

He blinked and glanced inside her car again. "I'll take your license and registration now."

"Yes, sir." She snatched her purse from the passenger seat to retrieve her license and then leaned over to grab the registration from the glovebox, all under his watchful eyes. She stood and held out her documents, hoping her friendly smile would ease the tension.

He showed no emotional reaction to her gesture and turned his attention to her driver's license. Then he flicked his gaze back to her. "Opal Mayland from Sedona, Arizona."

She tried a smile once more. "Yes."

He glanced between the license and her face, and then gave a curt nod. "Wait here, please."

With an unhurried swagger, he returned to his vehicle. She sagged against her damp car, and let the rain soothe her stress. Water was the least of her problems. She didn't need magic to know that things with Officer Keller hadn't gone well.

She could already hear a repeat of her grandfather's overused lecture on not driving as though the devil chased her. The thought of it tangled her nerves tighter. She was too old for him to take away her keys, but the disappointment in his eyes would be worse.

The sound of a car door closing drew her attention. Officer Keller sauntered back to her in an annoyingly confident manner. "Here you go, Ms. Mayland. Your record appears clean, with no outstanding warrants."

She could thank the stars for that. "Can I go, then?"

He chuckled. "Do you know how fast you were driving when I clocked you?"

Apparently, he'd accepted her explanation for not stopping, but she wasn't off the hook yet.

She considered his question. If she admitted she was speeding, he'd likely ticket her. Her only option was to continue to play innocent. "Uh...no. I didn't think I was going too fast."

He cleared his throat. "I clocked you at fourteen miles over the speed limit, and that was before you...panicked."

She sighed. "I'm sorry, officer, I didn't mean to speed. I've been driving for days, and I'm so ready to be out of the car. I was focused on my destination and didn't realize how fast I was going until I saw your lights."

Which was mostly true. She *did* like to drive fast, but she *had* been distracted.

He seemed interested in her response. "Are you visiting the area, then?"

Not exactly visiting, but she couldn't say she was a native to Crystal Cove without him asking questions about her family. With it being a small town, eventually he'd learn she was the chief's granddaughter, but hopefully, by then, the incident would have blown over.

"I'm headed to Crystal Cove."

He nodded in appreciation. "It's a beautiful town."

She answered with a smile. "I do love the ocean."

He relaxed his shoulders, giving her hope. "I'm going to do you a favor since you're visiting from Arizona. We wouldn't want you to get the wrong idea about the friendliness of Oregonians."

Thank the stars. He was going to let her off with a warning.

Instead, he held out a clipboard, and her short-lived happiness plummeted. "I've written the ticket for only nine miles over the limit, which should help your pocketbook considerably."

She swallowed her initial sarcastic response about him being too kind and swiped the clipboard from him.

He didn't seem to notice her small display of irritation. "Your signature is not an admittance of guilt. It only notes that you've received the citation. You have the option of appearing in court, or if you prefer to pay for your citation without contesting it, visit the website listed at the bottom."

She signed the paper with an annoyed flourish and shoved the clipboard toward him.

He tore off a copy of the ticket and handed it to her. "Take care out there, Ms. Mayland. Moisture on the roadways can make them slicker than normal."

So, she'd been told. "Yes, sir, Officer Keller."

He'd started to turn but paused when she used his name. He narrowed his eyes and then glanced to the name on his uniform and nodded. "Have a good day."

After he turned away, she rolled her eyes. Cops weren't the only ones who noticed details.

She climbed into her car, her clothes now damp enough to notice, and she sighed. This day was not turning out like she'd hoped at all. Her only wish was that he'd keep silent about the citation or not deem it worthy of conversation. After all, it was only one ticket out of plenty that he'd written.

CHAPTER TWO

O pal drove exactly the posted speed as she passed Crystal Cove's city limit sign and waited for the sense of home to surround her like a warm hug. When it came, her eyes welled with tears. She'd been gone too long and had forgotten exactly how much this town meant to her.

Except for her time in Sedona, she'd lived in the small oceanside village her whole life. Her mother and grandmother were buried in the cemetery at the top of the hill. She'd spent years running the halls of the old Victorian cottage her grandfather owned and countless hours reclaiming her mother's garden. Her best friend, Penelope, who'd been the only one to visit her in Sedona, still lived in the small house overlooking the ocean that had been in Penelope's family for years.

Of course, there were certain unfortunate things about her past years in Crystal Cove that she could never forget, either. Like how she'd walked the beach for days after her old boyfriend had crushed her heart, and how that had led to her asking to attend witch school out of state. Despite the fact that her grandfather had hunted paranormal beings and wasn't keen on any of them living in his town, he'd given his blessing. They'd both shed tears the day she'd left.

She'd grown during her time away, but she'd missed her friends and family. Not to mention the level of pure energy the town received from being sandwiched between the forests and the Pacific Ocean. Energy that could cleanse her spirit of the negativity that she'd received from her unfortunate encounter with that officer. Energy that would give her a sense of renewal and help her to restart her day in a positive way.

She fingered the moonstone pendant that had once been her mother's.

It always reminded her that as long as her heart continued to beat, she could start over. And there was no time like the present.

Instead of heading directly to the police station, where she'd likely find her grandfather, she turned on the first street at the edge of town, which led toward the ocean. She'd already intended to complete a small, personal ritual that night in her mother's garden, one that would mark the end of one leg of her journey. Then she could start the next with renewed hope and energy. But why wait?

Her car bumped along the uneven road that paralleled the fresh-water river winding its way to the salty ocean. When she spotted a grassy area, easy to reach from the street, she slowed and stopped alongside the Chemawa River.

She'd learned the power of a renewing ritual from her witch sisters not long after she'd arrived in Sedona. It had helped her to calm her fears about leaving her grandfather alone and helped to bury thoughts of her old boyfriend deep beneath the surface of her memories, where they wouldn't see the light of day.

The ritual was much like a meditation, but one where she invoked the power of the elements to help her. She tore a page from the small notebook she kept in her glovebox and wrote down her intentions and desires, which would focus her energy. Then she folded the paper into her palm and exited the car.

Delightful, addictive power accompanied the breeze rolling in from the ocean. It caressed her skin like a lover's kiss. She paused for a moment to soak it in and let the unseen energy soothe her soul. *This.* This was what she'd missed the most.

Many considered Crystal Cove nothing more than a small, seaside town, but she recognized the forces surging through the air. Strong, beautiful energy, freshly-cleansed by rain. Her grandfather always sensed it, too, but he preferred to think the magic belonged only to the ocean. At least he didn't deny that it was there.

She shut her car door and glanced about to see who else might be in the area. She wanted to focus on her emotions and connecting to nature without being disturbed. A maroon sedan sat parked on the opposite side, but thankfully, no one was around.

She opened the trunk, slid a small black case toward her, and extracted a fireproof ceramic bowl that she'd purchased in a pottery shop in Sedona. The gorgeous piece boasted swirls of red and burgundy and gave her a thrill every time she used it. With as wet as it was in Crystal Cove, it was unlikely she'd catch the grass on fire, but she liked to be careful.

Opal made her way toward the river. She created a path through the ankle-high grasses, down a gentle slope toward the river, and then walked until her senses told her she'd found the perfect spot.

Water flowed past in a lazy fashion, unaware of the cleansing turbulence that waited for it once it reached the vast ocean. She chose an open area amongst the twinberry and ninebark where she could see the river and sank to her knees before falling back on her bottom.

Moisture soaked through her jeans, but she didn't pay it much notice. She was already damp, and one couldn't live in a coastal town in Oregon and expect to stay dry.

She curled her legs to the side of her, placed the ceramic bowl in the grass, and closed her eyes. The sound of passing water calmed her senses. Deep breaths cleared any stress she'd carried from the long drive and allowed her to focus her thoughts.

When she was ready, she placed the paper with her written intentions inside the bowl. With a few whispered words, one corner of the paper caught fire. She cupped her hand along the side of the bowl to protect the swaying flame.

The tender flame grew as it consumed paper, and she held a hand out, allowing the heat to tickle her fingers. "I call to the element of Fire," she whispered.

The fire jumped, died low, and then jumped again, It circled the paper and turned it black as it released her hopes and desires into the universe.

When nothing was left but ashes, she pulled grass from the earth and lifted a pinch of soil. She rubbed the moist dirt between her thumb and forefinger and allowed it to fall into the bowl. "I call to the element of Earth."

She wasn't finished, but already, her soul felt lighter.

She exhaled the remnants of stress and stood, making her way to the edge of the riverbank. She poured the ashes and dirt into one hand and tossed them into the breeze. Some sank to the ground beneath her, while others caught the wind and drifted away into the water. "I call to the element of Air."

Carefully, she bent and scooped cool water into the bowl to wash away any remaining ashes, swirling her fingers around the edge before dumping it out. "I call to the element of Water."

She stood. "Great Goddess, hear my plea. Take negative energy away from me. Transform it into light and love. Grant these things from up above. This I ask, so mote it be."

A sense of calm filled her as she lifted her gaze to the sky. She was home and could be at peace now. The Goddess provided many beautiful things for her to enjoy and be thankful for. The fresh air. The gently flowing river, and—

The sight of something large bobbing in the water startled her, and she inhaled a quick breath. She fully expected to see a log or other debris, but that wasn't what was there at all.

Fear gripped her, and she took several clumsy steps backward. "A body," she said, barely able to breathe. "There's a body in the water."

CHAPTER THREE

Unfortunately, no one was around to hear Opal's declaration. She wanted to run but her legs wouldn't move. Instead, she gawked at the clearly lifeless form held in place by the thick bushes growing along the riverbank.

With her heart thumping violently, she glanced about, using her well-honed senses, searching for anyone who might harm her.

She found no black energy and nothing moved. For all she knew, the body could have been in there for hours. Days, even.

As the minutes passed, her better senses kicked in. She abandoned the body and hurried toward her car. Once there, she slipped the phone from her pocket and pressed buttons with shaking fingers to call her grandfather.

Sweet mother of pearl. This was not the way she'd planned to tell him she was back in town.

Several nerve-wracking rings echoed before he picked up. "Hello?"

The booming of her heart threatened to overwhelm her. "Hello, Grandpa."

"Opal? I'll be darned. How are things going down south?"

The familiar scratchiness of his voice and the words he'd spoken every time they'd talked comforted her. "I'm actually here, in Crystal Cove."

He snorted. "Stop pulling my leg."

Her emotions hovered between smiling at the sound of his voice and tearing up for the same reason. "No, I'm really here, but—"

He cleared his throat, cutting off her words. "Are you at the house?"

She'd thought he would sound more excited than he did. "No, I'm by the Ninth Street Bridge."

"The Ninth Street Bridge? What are you doing there?"

She inhaled a shaky breath. "Actually, I need you to come to me. You and your officers. I stopped for a second to..."

He wouldn't understand the ritual, and, right now, she didn't need him to.

"There's a body, Grandpa. A dead body in the river."

He paused. Then laughed. "Ah, little girl. You got me that time."

She swallowed, trying to maintain her grip on reality. "Grandpa, I wish I was kidding. I really am in Crystal Cove, and there really is a dead person. *I need you to come.*"

He didn't speak for what seemed like an eternity. Then he answered with a quick, "Be right there," and the line went dead.

She exhaled and pocketed her phone. Thank the Goddess.

Now that she knew he'd be there within minutes, her fears calmed, and her thoughts returned to the person floating in the river. She knew most of the residents in Crystal Cove, and she wondered if it was one of them, someone she knew. If not, perhaps someone from their neighboring town, Oceanview, or even a tourist.

Her grandpa would be there shortly, and as soon as he arrived, he'd make her leave. If she wanted to know the person's identity any time soon, now was her chance.

It was broad daylight, and she had a few protection spells she could invoke if needed. Call her crazy, but she headed back to the river.

She looked for trampled grass to see where she'd been before, and then moved farther east to where she could catch a glimpse of the body from a different perspective. She wouldn't get too close, but she wanted to see. Branches from the bushes tugged at her as she pushed her way through until the river was in clear view.

The face-down corpse bobbed only feet from her, and she gasped from the shock of it. She was much closer than she'd been before.

A man.

At least, he appeared to be if the size of his body, haircut, and clothing were good indicators, but she could only see the back of his head. His hair was short, his neck shaved, so she could safely assume he'd had it cut on a regular basis. Water sloshed against the light blue, long-sleeved shirt that she'd noticed earlier, and one of his shoes was missing.

"Bless your dearly departed soul," she whispered. "I hope you've lived a good life and that the heavens accept you."

The distant sound of emergency sirens filled the air, and Opal breathed easier. Help had almost arrived.

She made her way back through the bushes and up the slope to wait for her grandfather and his officers. Since her grandfather hadn't seen her in a while, maybe he wouldn't rush her off right away.

Crystal Cove's police chief was the first to arrive on scene, with two of his men screeching to a stop in SUVs right behind him. The sight of her grandpa at the wheel brought a quick, if not happy, smile to her face. He'd always been her hero.

The men killed their sirens and quickly exited. Her grandpa strode forward and reached her in seconds. Jeans, a tan police shirt, and a brown official Crystal Cove jacket covered the six-foot intimidating man. Strands of silver lightened his dark hair and goatee, but the intelligence in John Winston's eyes didn't waver.

"Where's the body?" he asked as he approached.

No warm hello. Not when business was at hand.

She pointed to the path she'd taken. "You can see him from there. He's a little upstream."

The chief nodded to his men. "You heard her. Pull him out."

Instead of following his men, he opened his arms. She folded herself into them and hugged him with all her heart. She'd missed him more than she'd realized.

He pulled back in an awkward manner and studied her. "Everything okay? It's not like you to show up without telling me."

She sent him a warm smile. He obviously didn't know her as well as he thought he did. "I wanted to surprise you."

He grunted. "This is a heck of a surprise."

She raised her brows in question. "Hopefully a good one?"

He hesitated for the briefest moment. "Of course, though we could have done without the dead body."

No doubt, the man was smart and cunning where law enforcement was concerned, but he could be as clueless as a pebble on the beach when it came to her. Growing up, she'd sometimes felt as if she was an oddity that he needed to study, that he needed to put in a box labeled with something he understood.

Problem was, she was something he would likely never understand.

But he loved her, so she forgave him for the caution he sometimes used with her. Paranormal hunters didn't normally love and try to understand witches. In his younger days, his parents had taught him to ask no questions and to erase all paranormal beings from the earth.

Her great grandparents were likely tossing in their graves.

Though she wasn't sure if they'd be more upset about her existence or that her grandpa had made a huge mistake when he'd unknowingly fallen in love with and married a witch. His only explanation was that love could make a man lose his mind. Though he'd worshipped her grandmother, he swore he'd never do it again.

Her grandfather called out orders as more responders arrived. The scene morphed into controlled chaos around them. He spent several minutes questioning her on what she'd seen, and she told him every detail she could remember.

Then he turned his gaze toward two officers, one male and one female, as they trudged up the grassy slope from the river. Betty Lou, a friend from high school, caught Opal's gaze and lifted her hand in a small wave before she turned toward the growing collection of arriving emergency vehicles.

Betty Lou had gone into law enforcement just like she'd said she would. Good for her.

Her counterpart, a guy with bright red hair and the last name Frank embroidered on his jacket, approached them and gave the police chief a grim look. "Dead alright. We're going to zip him straight out of the water, so we don't lose any possible evidence when we carry him up the hill."

Her grandpa nodded, a solemn expression on his face. "Good work, Derek. Can anyone I.D. him?"

Opal widened her eyes and held her breath.

Derek kept his gaze on his boss and released a heavy sigh. "Yes, sir. It's Jason Conrad."

Opal gasped.

Her grandpa cast a quick, admonishing glance at her before he spoke to Derek. "I feared it might be Jason when I spotted his car parked alongside the road back there. Hoped it would have been an outsider instead."

The news left her reeling. "Jason Conrad?" she said in a low voice. "He was an amazing swimmer in high school, even competed at the state level, remember?"

He turned to her with a pointed look. "Of course, I remember."

She lifted both hands, palms facing upward in question. "How could this happen? He wouldn't drown. Couldn't. Unless something bad happened to him that kept him from swimming."

The chief lifted his brows in warning. "That's why we investigate deaths, Opal."

The tone he used stung. He followed up with a look that suggested she should be a silent bystander, and that, technically, she shouldn't be privy to any details of Jason's death until they were released publicly.

Then he turned back to Derek. "Let's get him loaded and out of here."

Derek nodded and trailed after Betty Lou. Opal guessed that he meant to help her with the body bag and whatever items were needed to do their job. She found herself mildly jealous that Betty Lou could be involved. Not that she wanted to touch a dead body, though.

CHAPTER FOUR

A mass of activity encapsulated the area like angry bees swarming a hive. Opal stayed quiet and watched, hoping that if she did so, she could remain on the scene longer. Watching the officers work fascinated her in a way that it hadn't when she'd been younger.

She caught movement in her periphery and turned.

Big and beefy, Patrol Sergeant Hank Halverson strode toward them. "John, you gotta—"

Hank paused when he caught sight of her. His thick blond mustache and beard nearly covered his smile. "Didn't expect to see you here, Opal."

The man created a whirlwind of energy wherever he went. She figured it was because he occupied more space than most people. She'd also decided years ago that it was a good thing he wasn't an introvert, because, with his stature and presence, he'd never be able to pull off being the quiet one in the corner.

Hank had a warm heart and never showed his fierce side to the good folks in town. At least, not that she'd seen. Nevertheless, she'd heard stories about his behavior when criminals weren't so nice, and she felt bad for whoever ended up on the bad side of his fist.

She grinned. "Hey, Hank. It's good to see you."

"Good to see you, too. I hope that you're home to stay."

She nodded. "I am."

Her grandpa flashed her a questioning look as though he was surprised by her answer.

Hank interrupted before her grandpa could comment. "Moretti needs you, Chief."

Her grandpa didn't leave, but instead, he leaned close to Hank with a serious look. "Think that siren might be responsible?" he asked in a low voice.

Sirens?

His question stoked the fires of curiosity inside her. As far as she knew, sirens, the mystical nymphs of the sea, supposedly preferred to keep to warmer waters, not the chilly ocean of the Pacific Northwest. And that was if they were even real.

She studied her grandfather, wondering if he was the one now joking around with her. It wouldn't be the first time he and Hank had done something similar.

"Could be," Hank responded in a conspiratorial tone. "Ernie's not one to make up fish stories. You know, it's only a matter of time before they cast a spell over some unfortunate soul."

She narrowed her gaze in disgust, now knowing that they were teasing her. Sirens did *not* cast spells. Witches did. Sirens lured men to their deaths with beautiful songs. Instead of calling them on their ruse, she decided to play along. "You think a siren killed him?"

Hank and her grandpa both shushed her.

Her grandpa took her by the elbow. "We don't discuss such matters in voices loud enough that others can hear, remember?"

She rolled her eyes. Her grandfather freaked whenever anything paranormal, real or imagined, popped up in a conversation. "Yes, I remember."

Satisfied with her response, her grandpa nodded, and he and Hank stepped away from her. "Let's see what Moretti needs."

She followed a few feet behind.

Before they went very far, her grandpa paused and narrowed his eyes. "This is a murder investigation, Opal. You don't need to see a dead body."

She frowned, not wanting to be left out. "I've already seen it. I found him, remember?"

Her grandfather shook his head in disagreement. "It's different seeing someone floating face down in the water than it is to see the swollen, distorted features once we pull him out. I need to get busy, and you need to go. Stop by the station to give a written statement."

She hesitated. "I thought maybe I could help. An extra set of eyes doesn't hurt anything, and I'm...smarter than I was before I left for Arizona."

She wanted to remind him that she'd left to hone her witchcraft and that those skills might come in handy. But that wouldn't go over very well.

The ashen look on his face told her that he'd understood, anyway. He put a firm hand on her shoulder. "In a police investigation, everything has to be by the book."

Meaning, no magic. Still, he'd let her know in not so many words that he thought it might be murder, too.

He dropped his hand and cleared his throat. "You've always told me you were like your grandma and wanted nothing to do with my job."

That was sort of true. In the past, she'd fallen prey to empathizing with victims and their families, to the point that it would keep her awake at night or give her nightmares.

She still sensed people's feelings, but she'd learned to close herself off when needed. She shrugged. "I don't know. Maybe I'm more like you than I'd realized, especially now that I'm older."

He snorted. "Are you saying you want to hunt criminals like witches and demons?" he asked in a low voice.

She might have thought it was a threat, but she knew her grandfather better than that. She leaned close to whisper, hoping he could understand her point of view. "Not every police officer chases paranormal beings. There are plenty of regular criminals out there. Besides, we don't hunt witches, remember?"

Color returned to his cheeks, and he straightened to his full height. "I hunt whatever causes problems for the town, Opal. If anyone, and I mean anyone, stirs up trouble, I'll bring 'em down."

Something about the way he looked at her when he said it made her wonder if he'd included her in that statement. She *was* an adult now. He might hold her to different standards. Perhaps that was why he'd given her that look when she'd told Hank she was back to stay.

Then she pushed that ridiculous thought aside. Even if he seemed a little off, he was her grandpa, the one who'd been there for her ever since her mother and grandmother had tragically died. Time and distance couldn't affect that.

Their conversation had gotten way off track. "I just think that detective work sounds interesting."

He patted her shoulder, and she sensed his patience growing thin. "Dealing with criminals, paranormal or otherwise, is no place for my granddaughter. You need to find a nice, quiet, safe job. Work at the vet's office. Or how about being a nanny for the Alexander's. I've heard they're looking. Or better yet, go back to Sedona. You're safer there."

She tilted her head. Perhaps he really didn't want her back in Crystal Cove. The thought that it could be true cut her deeply.

He drew his brows together, and she sensed the conflict in his soul. He *was* happy to see her, but there was something else at play.

"He's right," Hank interrupted. "A crime scene is no place for a young lady."

She exhaled and buried her retort. There was no way she could argue with them both. "Don't worry about me. Go do your job."

Her grandpa gave her a half smile. "You could visit Eleanor. I know she'd love to see you."

She lifted her chin in half-hearted agreement and turned away.

Eleanor? She hadn't come all the way home to see his housekeeper. She did know her because Eleanor had worked for her grandfather for a year before Opal had headed to Arizona, but the woman had never been especially warm with her. Though that wasn't necessarily a reason to dislike a person. Eleanor wasn't mean. But still, his housekeeper?

Disappointment trailed along with her as she headed toward her car. She supposed her grandpa had been right to send her on her way, but she hoped that someday he could see the value of her insight and magic.

Thoughts of Jason's mom and sister crowded in. Their world had been upended, and they didn't even know it yet. The thought saddened her. His mom, Bonnie had always been a huge supporter of Jason's. She'd talked non-stop of his accomplishments the year he'd gone to the state championships.

Opal would like to think Jason's death would bother his sister, Sally, too, even though the two had never been close. Perhaps offering the family a shoulder to cry on would be the only way she'd be able to help with his death. And that held value, too.

She sighed, resigned to her fate for now.

She called her best friend, Penelope, to see if she could stop by for a visit. Unfortunately, the call went straight to voicemail, so she left a message, hoping they could connect later.

Maybe, she'd head to the center of town and order up a big fat serving of fish and chips at Malcolm's Diner. There, perhaps, she'd finally get the welcome she craved.

As she neared her car, she eyed the off-limits maroon sedan parked across the street that apparently belonged to Jason. Her curiosity burned, but she couldn't do anything that would disturb the car. She needed to let the police do their jobs.

Although...it couldn't hurt to take a quick look inside through the windows, could it? She wouldn't touch anything. She just wanted a peek.

She glanced toward the group of officers down the street and then strode closer. She shut out surrounding energy and peered inside the driver's window, wishing she could intuit what had taken place between the moment Jason had left that spot and when he'd ended up in the river.

Nothing came to her.

Still, unless Jason had been inebriated or some such thing, which she highly doubted because he'd always been a fitness freak, she couldn't picture him drowning. He'd been a state champion swimmer, for goodness sake.

Murdered.

The word filtered through her mind. It seemed very plausible. Even her grandfather had thought the same. Perhaps someone hated Jason enough to kill him. Or maybe it had been a robbery gone wrong. If she'd been inside a building, she might have picked up on negative energies, but here, ocean breezes quickly whisked away any remaining metaphysical evidence.

Disappointed by the lack of anything interesting, she stepped away. No one needed to tell her that standing and staring inside his car windows wouldn't give her the answers she sought. As stubborn as she could be at times, she knew a lost cause when she saw it. She'd be better off stuffing her face with fish and chips.

She turned and headed toward her car.

Several steps later, an eerie sensation cascaded over her. The feeling was strong enough to cause her to pause and look around, and she wondered if magic was at play somehow.

She hesitated for a few moments, trying to sense something further. Nothing registered, so she shrugged it off and kept walking.

Then a second attack on her senses raised unexpected goosebumps on her skin, and this time, she knew she couldn't ignore the prompting. She glanced around again, wondering what she was missing. She wished desperately that she'd been gifted a familiar like all her friends in Sedona had, one who might provide an alternate perspective to help her figure things out.

But the Great Goddess hadn't gifted her that way, and she'd begun to doubt she ever would. Most witches had found their companion at a much younger age than she was. Of course, most witches had had a different upbringing than her, too. Either way, she'd accepted she'd be practicing as a solitary witch.

Still, she could find nothing out of the ordinary, which left her wondering if maybe she'd been hexed. The uneasy feeling reminded her of the time an adversary in Sedona had placed one on her. But who would do that to her in Crystal Cove? Her grandfather had done a fantastic job of keeping all other witches away. Though he did seem tolerant, albeit dismissive, of Penelope's claim of coming from a family of psychics. In his opinion, psychics were just people making up stories.

When she was about to give up, a flash of metal lying amongst the thicker native grasses near the sidewalk snagged her attention and sent her pulse racing. Perhaps that was the cause of the disturbance around her. She strode closer, and found a silver pendant nestled deep in the grass.

Not just any pendant, but an infinity heart, a vow of never-ending love. It seemed innocuous enough at first, but the longer she stared, the more she wondered. Only one end of the chain was visible, but the clasp was clearly broken. But had someone broken the clasp through a violent tug, or had someone discarded it because it had been ruined by some other means?

However, she couldn't ignore that there was a possibility that it was connected to Jason's death. She probably should point it out to her grandfather, but she feared how the next few moments would go. She'd report her finding and risk having him berate her for not having left yet.

To leave would be the easiest option.

Unfortunately, she couldn't stay quiet and hope his men would find the necklace. It might have nothing to do with the investigation, but it also might provide an important clue. She straightened her spine and prepared for an unhappy grandfather.

CHAPTER FIVE

Opal inhaled a fortifying breath and headed toward the center of chaos. She should be celebrating her homecoming with her grandpa, not dealing with a dead person.

As she neared the crime scene, the chief met her gaze with a frown. "I thought you were going to visit Eleanor."

She didn't want to discuss Eleanor. Instead, she thumbed over her shoulder toward Jason's car. "There's something in the grass over there. A broken pendant."

He glanced in that direction, and Opal detected a hint of irritation vibrating from him. "Okay."

She lifted a shoulder and let it drop. "I thought it might be connected to Jason's death."

He stared at her for a long moment. "It might. We will get to the surrounding area and his car. But first things first."

She knew that, but it seemed that since she'd found something, he or one of his men should collect it now. "So, you don't want me to point it out?"

"Let me do my job, Opal."

She didn't understand the traces of animosity that emanated from him. She hadn't done anything wrong, so why was he acting like she had? If she didn't know better, she'd swear he was a different man from the one who'd raised her. "If I could walk past and look at it, who's to stop anyone else from doing the same and picking it up?"

He expelled a deep breath and swiveled toward the group of people trying to complete their work. "Where's Lucas?" he called.

A dark-haired officer stepped from behind a group of first responders. "I'm here."

Opal inhaled a sharp breath.

Not again.

The sight of Officer Keller walking toward them whisked away the last vestiges of hope she'd had for a good day. She didn't know how or when he'd arrived on scene, and now, she wished she hadn't stopped to investigate that odd sensation.

She and her grandfather were already rubbing each other wrong, like sand stuck beneath a swimming suit. If Lucas mentioned their earlier encounter, that would only make things worse.

His gaze swept over her as he approached, and she caught the flicker of surprise in his eyes. He blinked and shifted his attention to his boss. "What's up?"

The chief pointed toward Jason's car. "Take an evidence bag and walk down the street with this young lady. She's spotted a possible piece of evidence that we need to collect *right away*."

Interest flashed in his eyes. "Will do, Chief."

"Afterward," her grandfather continued. "Escort my granddaughter to her car and make sure that she gets safely on her way."

Irritation and embarrassment flared inside her. She didn't need an escort to her car, and she didn't need him to talk about her in a way that humiliated her in front of his officers.

She wanted to cry foul, but the police chief had spoken with an authoritative voice that made it very clear that neither she nor Officer Keller should argue. She wouldn't embarrass her grandpa like he'd done to her. However, she would bring it up that night at dinner.

"Your granddaughter?" Lucas asked the chief as he was walking away.

"Yeah," he called over his shoulder. "While you're at it, cordon off this whole block. I don't want anyone else unofficial entering the area."

Anyone else unofficial? That's how he thought of her? Her grandpa seemed to have forgotten she was the one who'd discovered the body and called in the crime. He also seemed to have forgotten that family came first, and he should treat her with kindness.

Lucas gave a quick nod. "Will do."

She turned and strode away. Officer Keller quickly fell in step next to her. Neither of them said a word as she led him toward the pendant, and she wondered if he felt as awkward as she did.

He was at least six feet tall, if not more, and she was hyperaware of how he towered over her. Of how his long-legged gait forced her to walk faster to keep up with him. The worst was his intense green eyes that seemed to see right through her.

She wished she could gain the same insight about him, but all she sensed was his mellow demeanor. Gone was any surprise from seeing her again. If he was annoyed that he had to stop his work to accommodate the request to help her, she didn't sense a bit of it. In fact, she realized that she picked up little emotion from him at all.

Perhaps his calm collectedness was a skill he'd honed as an officer. One that would likely come in handy in his line of duty.

Even so, she wondered what was going through his mind. It seemed they were not going to discuss their earlier encounter where he'd ticketed her for speeding. Which was totally fine.

Still, as the moments ticked by, it became more awkward that they weren't saying anything to each other. She considered mentioning the weather to break the ice, but she couldn't bring herself to do it.

When they neared Jason's car, he paused and turned to her.

She glanced at him with questioning eyes, wondering why he was staring at her so intensely.

He lifted curious brows. "Are you going to show me the evidence?"

His question ripped her from her thoughts, and her cheeks heated. She needed to stay focused. "Right over here."

Opal led him to where the shiny, twisted heart lay nestled in the grass and pointed to it.

He took time to photograph the area from different angles, including several close-up shots and a few more that showed where the necklace lay in proximity to its surroundings. Then he opened a plastic evidence bag, turned it inside out to use as a glove, and picked up the necklace. He flipped the bag again and zipped the evidence inside.

When he finished, he lifted his gaze to her. The color of his eyes reminded her of the leaves from an alder tree, vibrant and full of energy.

She hesitated for a moment, unsure of whether she should speak or if he had something on his mind. "Is that all?" she finally asked.

He gazed at her for several long, uncomfortable seconds. "Unless you have something else to show me."

She shook her head several times. "Nope. That's it."

He gave her a curt nod. "I trust that you can find your way to your car and that you won't speed when you leave."

His comment brought her irritation from the morning's events to a head. "Are you going to arrest me if I stay?"

He snorted. "I might. To be honest, I'm curious why you're at the scene in the first place."

She sure as heck wouldn't tell him about her ritual. "I stopped to look at the river and found the body."

"Why?"

She lifted her brows in surprise. "Why did I stop? Because I wanted to. Do I need to have a better reason than that?"

He studied her, giving her an anxious feeling. "Why didn't you tell me who you were earlier? It's not smart to lie to an officer."

She shot him an appalled look. "I didn't lie. I told you my real name, and there's not a law that says I have to disclose the names of my family."

He narrowed his gaze. "It would have been nice to know my boss is your grandfather."

She shrugged. "Are you saying I should have used my family's influence to avoid a ticket?"

He dipped his head. "Most people would. Besides, you're assuming that I would have let you off."

She folded her arms. "Are you saying you wouldn't have?"

He studied her for a long uncomfortable moment before a spark of knowing flashed in his eyes. A half-smile curved his lips. "Oh, I get it. You didn't say anything because you don't want him to know that you'd been caught speeding."

Apparently, insight was another irritating trait he'd honed. "My grandpa doesn't need to know every aspect of my life. He runs enough in this town. He doesn't need to run me."

Opal knew her sass came from how her grandfather had treated her, but she couldn't help it. Everything in Crystal Cove seemed off kilter, and she didn't need this man making her life grittier.

Officer Keller lifted his chin in acknowledgement. "Hmm...sounds like you've clashed with the chief before over speeding."

She shot an annoyed glance heavenward but didn't respond to his comment. "Are we finished here?"

His soft chuckle drew her gaze to him. "I'm right. Aren't I?"

She wished she could hate him, but there was something about the man that intrigued her. Still, she'd had enough friction for the day. "It sounds to me like this is a matter best kept between us. You caught me in a moment of weakness, when I wasn't paying attention to the speed limit. No one is perfect."

The look in his eyes said he questioned if that was the complete truth. But it was all the truth he needed to know.

"You were just doing your job," she continued. "It happened, and my grandfather has nothing to do with it. I'll pay my fine, and that will be the end of it. Deal?"

Officer Keller regarded her for a long moment and then a hint of a smile curved his lips. "Deal."

He stuck out a hand for her to shake, and her annoyance eased. This was an acceptable solution, even if she didn't particularly care for the man. She slid her hand into his to seal the deal.

Strange, dark energy shot straight to her heart, and she gasped at the unexpected sensation.

He pulled his hand away, seeming as unnerved as she was. A second later, that emotion was gone. "You need to leave, and I need to get back to work."

With that, he turned without waiting for her response and strode away.

She stared after him, dumbfounded. She had no idea what had just happened. But something had.

The sensation she'd gotten from him hadn't been electrical, but she wasn't sure how else to describe it. Odd. Definitely. And powerful.

Despite all that, his touch had given her what she'd wanted. A bit of an insight into his soul. Something lurked beneath the surface, and it was far different from the cool, calm exterior he presented to the world.

Something darker lingered inside him, and she yearned to discover exactly what that might be. She curved her lips into a small smile. It appeared that she wasn't the only one in town with a secret, and suddenly, Crystal Cove held more interest than it had only hours before.

Maybe she couldn't be involved with investigating Jason Conrad's death, but she'd certainly be delving more into Officer Lucas Keller. In fact, she'd start by pondering their interactions over a delicious basket of Malcolm's fish and chips.

CHAPTER SIX

The second Opal stepped inside Malcolm's Diner, she finally felt like she'd come home. Maybe she'd had a moment of that welcoming feeling when her grandfather had hugged her, but that had quickly dissolved into frustration.

But here, with the scents of fries and fresh yeasty donuts, she knew she'd arrived.

Lunchtime had passed, and dinner was hours away, so the place was mostly empty. Perfect for her.

She seated herself, as per the sign at the front, and leaned back against the wooden booth. She'd chosen the same spot where she and her best friend Penelope had always sat so that they could keep an eye on any interesting guys who might walk past.

As high school students, she and Penelope had often popped in after classes to share a basket of fries and chug down sodas, well-known staples of Crystal Cove teens. It seemed like only yesterday that she'd been here with her friend, where they'd often laughed so hard that they'd cried.

A deep chuckle sounded from behind her, and she turned.

Malcolm Harris's brown eyes warmed when their gazes met, and he grinned. More gray had infiltrated his short, black corkscrew curls, but he still seemed as young and spry as ever. "Well, if it ain't Miss Opal come home to see us at last. What's kept you away for so long?"

She stood and threw her arms around his neck in a fierce hug. Malcolm had been her friend since she'd been a little girl, and he'd always been someone who'd listened and offered friendly advice.

She pulled back and met his gaze. "Don't be silly. You know I was away at school."

He scoffed. "For six years? And not one visit? Could have come home for Christmas."

She felt bad that she never had. "I'm sorry I didn't get back here during the holidays. It was complicated and things never seemed to work out with my grandpa for whatever odd reason, but just know, I missed all of you so much."

He shook his head, letting her know the full breadth of his disappointment.

She smiled, hoping to tease him out of his sour mood. "I did email you. A lot."

He flicked a dismissive hand toward her. "I told you not to expect me to read them. You know that internet stuff goes over my head."

That or he was too stubborn to learn. "But I showed you how it works, Malcolm. You turn on the computer. Open your email account. It's not hard."

This time, he waved away her comments with both hands. "I know what you said. But it doesn't work. Nia helped me the first time, so I did read that one email, but that computer nonsense belongs to your generation. I'm fine without it."

Opal wanted to point out that if he'd tried, they would have stayed better connected. She would have loved to hear about the happenings in Crystal Cove from his perspective.

She sighed, knowing that trying to convince him was a losing battle. "Well, I'm home now. Home to stay."

He narrowed his gaze in a half-trusting way but shook his head again.

"I feel like my grandpa needs me," she added for good measure.

He tipped his head in agreement to that statement. "Man's gotta be getting ready for retirement, I'd think."

She chuckled. Malcolm was older than he was and nowhere near retirement, either. "I don't know if he'll ever slow down enough for that."

Malcolm snorted, and a warm sense of love enveloped her. Despite his words, she knew he was as excited to see her as she was to see him. "You know, other than my grandpa, you're the first person I came to see. I've only been home a little over an hour."

"Don't try to butter me up now. I know the only reason you're in here is 'cause of my fish and chips. If it weren't for them, I'd hardly see you at all."

Part of that was true. Years ago, she'd come for the delicious food, but she and Penelope had soon made friends with the older man, and Opal had found him to be a great mentor, especially when her grandfather wasn't available.

She nodded toward the opposing side of the table. "Can you sit with me?"

He chuckled, and she sensed she'd been forgiven. "Let me get Jerry started on your order, and then I will. The usual?"

She grinned and nodded. "Man, how I've missed our conversations."

He winked. "Be right back. I'm looking forward to hearing about your adventures."

Malcolm returned a few moments later carrying a glass filled to the brim with ice and soda. He set it before her and then claimed the seat opposite.

She carefully sipped it before she spilled.

Malcolm slapped his hands face down on the table in a dramatic gesture. "Let's hear all about your so-called education."

It was her turn to shake her head in consternation, though her smile remained. Malcolm was one of the few people in Crystal Cove who knew she was a witch. Knew that her grandfather had agreed to let her go with the hope that she could learn skills so that if any hunters found her, she could protect herself.

She had no idea how to condense everything she'd learned into a few concise words. "It was interesting. Most of the witches were very nice, very helpful. A few were prickly, but I didn't have any real issues with them."

"Sounds like a regular group of people."

She snorted softly. "Yeah, except they can hex you if they don't like you."

He widened his eyes. "Did you learn how to do that, too?"

She grinned, enjoying the fact that she now understood the energy vibrating beneath her skin. "I could if I wanted to, but hexing is serious business. It has the potential to bring about bad karma."

He drew his lips into a pucker and shook his head. "Oh, no. Don't be messing with that. My grandma grew up in Louisiana, and she knew all about voodoo priestesses who hexed and cursed people. Dangerous stuff, for sure."

For the many hours they'd talked during her life, he'd never mentioned voodoo. "Are you serious?"

"Sure am. That was the main reason she and her family hid on a shrimp boat and hightailed it out of the area. One of them priestesses thought my gran had wronged her. Apparently, out of sight, out of mind was the only defense she'd had."

The man had a way with stories, and the images he'd created over the years remained vivid in her head. "That's crazy."

His voice rose with excitement. "The priestess was the crazy one."

"But your grandma got away without trouble?"

He nodded. "I think so. My mother told me she'd come down with a serious rash only days after they'd left. But it went away, and all was well."

"I'm sure that was a relief for the whole family."

The thought of relatives brought back Jason's murder, and she wondered if the police had notified his mother yet.

"You got some worry settling in your eyes," Malcolm said. "What's up?"

The man had a keen sense of the emotions of others, too. "A lot of things. I need a job before my grandpa tells the Alexanders that I'll be their nanny. He still treats me like I'm eighteen. And..." She drew out the word as disturbing images of Jason's body flashed through her mind.

"And?" he prompted.

Opal leaned toward the center of the table. "Don't say anything because I don't know that the official word is out yet, but I found a body floating in the Chemawa River, right after I arrived in Crystal Cove."

He exhaled and leaned back. "Lord, have mercy. Who was it?"

"Jason Conrad," she said quietly.

"Jason?" he said louder than he should, though there wasn't anyone around to hear. "Why, that boy is a good swimmer. Top in his class."

She gave him a solemn look. "I know."

He looked at her more carefully. "And *you* found him?"

She nodded. "I stopped to do a refreshing ritual right after I arrived in Crystal Cove. I wanted to make sure I was starting fresh with no baggage."

Though that hadn't worked out so well.

He murmured in understanding. "That's going to kill his mama."

She sighed. "I know. I wish someone else would have found Jason. I like Bonnie, and I don't want to be tangled up in her heartbreak."

Malcolm shifted in his seat and then shook his head. "I can't believe it would be an accident. I've watched that guy, and he could swim. He's the last person in this town that would drown."

At last, someone who would discuss the incident and not shut her down. "Right? I think my grandpa is not giving that enough consideration."

He snorted. "More likely he is, but he's not sharing it with you."

Opal sagged against the seat. "Yeah. You're probably right."

Malcolm rolled his shoulders and then leaned closer to her, resting his forearms on the table. "Bet you anything Jason's ex-wife has something to do with it."

Her curiosity perked like the ears on a nervous cat. "He'd gotten married then, while I was away?"

He nodded. "Yep. To Kandace Grisby a few years back. They have a son, Beau."

She lifted her brows in surprise. "Kandace? I can't see Jason risking his precious golden boy reputation to date her. She was like a quiet mouse."

Malcolm chortled. "*Was* is the keyword. She completely transformed herself. Looks like an uppity beauty queen these days. *He* was lucky she'd date him. Wouldn't be surprised if she'd finally had enough of him."

Opal nodded, intrigued by his description of Kandace. "Guess I'll have to figure out a way to stop in and say hi. I'd be curious to see what kind of vibes she puts off these days."

They paused in conversation while Jerry brought food to the table.

Opal smiled warmly at the short, skinny cook. It was true that the best chefs weren't always pudgy. Then she turned her attention to the golden fried cod and a huge pile of tater tots. Jerry always did take good care of her. "This looks heaven sent. Thank you."

Jerry beamed and dipped his head in approval. "Good to see you again, little girl."

He turned and disappeared behind the two-way swinging door into the kitchen.

Opal dipped a tot in ketchup and plopped it into her mouth. Crispy deliciousness delighted her taste buds. "Oh, dang. I really should have come home sooner."

"Uh-huh," Malcolm said and grinned.

She paused to enjoy a bite of fish dipped in tartar sauce and then focused on Malcolm and the other question burning in her mind. "How long has Officer Keller been in town?"

CHAPTER SEVEN

Malcolm shot Opal a pointed look across the wooden table that separated them. "You mean *Assistant Police Chief* Keller. He's far more than an officer."

Opal pinched her expression as though she'd just bitten a sour cherry. "*Assistant?* That makes no sense. If grandpa was going to promote someone to help him, he'd pick Hank."

"I'm not sure he was given the choice. The mayor might have had something to do with it."

Her suspicions grew. "Mayor Kaplinski forced Keller on him? Is she blackmailing him?"

The older man shook his head. "Not blackmail. At least not the version you're thinking of."

He leaned in close. "There was an issue a while back that may or may not have damaged your grandfather's reputation. Not with the people, mind you. Everyone in Crystal Cove loves him. But..."

Her curiosity exploded. "What happened?"

He shook his head. "Not my place to say. But I will tell you that shortly after that, we found ourselves with a brand-new assistant police chief."

"Come on, Malcolm. I should know about this if it affects my grandpa."

Malcolm shook his head.

Stubborn man. She knew him well enough to know that pressing him further would do no good. Instead, she returned her thoughts to the assistant chief, and her suspicions of him grew. "So, Keller is the mayor's spy, then."

"No, I wouldn't say that. Lucas Keller isn't a spy. He's his own man, and a good one, too."

She snorted. "That's still up for debate. How long ago did they hire him?"

She'd been a thousand miles away and hadn't realized her grandfather had needed support. The thought weighed heavy, and she reaffirmed that it was good that she'd come home.

Malcolm lifted his gaze skyward as though that would help him access his memory. "Well, let's see. Lucas came right before Amanda Reid had her baby because he had to rush her to the hospital while she was in labor. Amanda's boy is about three, so Lucas's been here a while I guess."

She nodded and sipped her soda.

Malcolm gave her a sly smile. "Despite his position as Assistant Police Chief, do I sense another reason for your interest in him?"

She shrugged. "No reason. Met him this morning and wondered."

A sly grin crossed his lips. "Uh-huh. If I were to guess, I'd think it's more than that, especially knowing how crazy you and Penelope always were for the boys. Lucas Keller is a fine-looking man."

She shook her head repeatedly. "That was a long time ago, Malcolm. I've learned my lesson as far as men are concerned."

His eyes glittered with laughter. "Leopards don't change their spots. I'd say someone like you might find him attractive."

She choked on a swallow and then coughed to clear her throat. "Hardly. Officer Friendly gave me a ticket on my way into town, and honestly, I found him kind of odd."

The realization that she'd confessed her sin stopped her short. "Wait. Don't tell my grandpa about the ticket, okay?"

A chuckle rumbled from within him. "You know our conversations are always private. So, you were speeding again, huh? Can't say I'm surprised."

She opened her hands in a show of innocence. "I don't speed...all the time."

He shot her a look that said he hadn't been born yesterday. "Right."

She flattened her palms against the table in protest. "I don't. I go slow in the zones around houses and kids. Where it matters."

"You know, I would say a ticket might teach you a lesson, but we both know that ain't true."

He laughed, and she rolled her eyes. Instead of commenting, she lifted a tater tot and dunked it in ketchup.

He grinned, knowing he'd pushed her buttons. "You mentioned a job. You know you could work here."

She snorted. "You'd fire me after the first day, and you know it. I'd get frustrated and accidentally dump someone's salad in their lap."

He grinned. "Probably so. Then what is it you'd like to do?"

Her dreams danced to life once again. "I'd really like to help the police department with my new skills. I'm sure I could be an asset, but my grandpa won't allow it. So, I've also dreamed about opening a shop here in town."

"A shop?" he asked with interest. "What kind of shop? Jewelry? Clothes?"

She allowed her thoughts to drift into her dream. "Actually, I was thinking a metaphysical shop."

He drew his brows together. "Is that so?"

"Yeah, a kind of magical or spiritual place. I'd carry many things that a witch might use, but the items would also make great souvenirs for those uneducated in the supernatural. Things like incense and crystals. I could do jewelry, scarves, homemade paper, letter openers. Maybe I could even hire a psychic to do readings for people."

Malcolm seemed to consider her ideas. "Not bad. There's plenty of tourists willing to part with a few bucks in order to take a piece of Crystal Cove home with them."

Her outlook brightened. "Exactly. Crystals from Crystal Cove. The only problem is, I'm not sure how much money I'd need to get started."

He nodded grimly. "It's always the money."

She bit her bottom lip, not deterred by his statement. "Plus, I'm not sure I'm ready to tackle something so big, but maybe someday soon. I need to get settled first."

"How's your grandpa going to react to that idea?"

She shrugged. "Probably not well, but I'm an adult, and I get to make my own choices."

"Uh-huh. All right. Well, in the meantime, Miss Marla is hiring."

Opal straightened. "At the Rosewood Inn? I love that place. It's supposed to be haunted, you know."

He smiled and stood. "Could be. Finish eating, walk over, and talk to her. Might be just the thing you're looking for right now."

He gestured toward a group of six who'd just entered the diner. They glanced around looking lost, obviously unable to read the seat-yourself sign. "I best take care of my customers."

She gave him a wide smile. "Thanks, Malcolm. You always make everything better."

"Uh-huh," he said and sauntered off.

Ten minutes later, Opal left Malcolm's diner with her stomach uncomfortably full. Yet, she couldn't regret enjoying those crispy little tots and amazing fish. If she didn't know better, she'd say Malcolm crafted food with magic.

Her dark ponytail swung as she headed toward the ocean, along a sidewalk pitted by salt and weather. Somber gray clouds hovered overhead, letting the occasional ray of sunshine through. Today should be a solemn day, she decided. Someone had died, and it seemed wrong to hope for full sun.

The beginnings of a headache had set in by the time she neared the boardwalk that separated businesses and hotels from the beach. When the full force of ocean winds greeted her, blowing loose strands of her hair back from her face, she inhaled the salt-kissed air and sighed. The breeze cleansed her soul like nothing else.

Opal's phone rang and stole her attention. She pulled it from her pocket, read the screen, and stiffened. Her grandpa.

Tension vibrated between her temples.

"Hello?" Opal said cautiously. She was still angry with him for how he'd treated her.

"Where are you?" His deep voice boomed across the phone line. "I need you at the station," he said before she could answer his question.

"I'm not far from the Rosewood Inn."

"Oh?" he said, changing his tone to an interested one. "Are you applying for the job there? I've heard she's hiring."

Geez, give a girl a minute. "That's where I was headed."

"Good, but I need you to come to the station first. I need a written statement from you."

A heavy sigh slipped from her lips before she could stop it. "I'll head there now."

"Good. And leave the attitude behind."

She clicked off her phone and stared at it. *What was up with him?*

He'd already taken a detailed oral statement, and they both knew the written one could wait a while longer. But with her grandfather, everything was urgent.

She switched directions and headed toward her car. She'd drive it the couple of blocks from Malcolm's to the station. She could walk, but the day was wearing on her, and she wished she could tell her grandfather to lose his attitude, too.

On the sidewalk ahead of her, corpses of plants that had outlived the winter season lay withered in a pile. Sadly, she identified with them.

The city's beautification project paid to have Main Street's pocket gardens kept in top condition and an enviable source of beauty for the town's visitors. A good use of tax dollars if anyone asked her.

A woman with short brown hair shot with gray stood, appearing from behind a dense boxwood shrub, surprising Opal. She brushed dirt from her overalls. The woman had been kneeling on the street side, so Opal hadn't noticed her until she was almost upon her.

When Opal's gaze connected with hers, she realized she knew the woman.

Bonnie Conrad. Good grief. *Jason's mother.*

The unwelcome throb in her temple that had begun with her grandpa's call spiked with intensity.

Bonnie greeted her with a warm smile. "Opal Mayland? Is that you?"

Judging by the look on Bonnie's face, Opal knew for certain that no one had told her what had happened to her son. She ignored the increased pounding in her head and forced herself to smile. "Hello, Bonnie. I didn't recognize you at first."

A knowing twinkle sparkled in her eyes. "That's because the last time I saw you, I was much younger, with long hair and not a trace of gray."

Thoughts of Jason's death invaded Opal's thoughts and sickened her stomach. "Maybe so."

The poor woman had no idea her world had turned upside down, and Opal was a fraud standing there, carrying on small chitchat, as if everything was okay. She ached from withholding information and wished she could gently tell Bonnie what had happened. But it wasn't her place to interfere with police business.

"Back in town to stay?" Bonnie continued, a perfect example of the infamous small-town friendliness that Crystal Cove was known for.

Opal found herself in a terrible trap. The next time Bonnie saw her, she would know that Opal had found her son, that they'd had this conversation, and that she'd said nothing. She might hold that against her. "I am. Just got back this morning, and, unfortunately, it's been an awful day."

Flashes of light in her vision warned that a monstrous headache was imminent, and her day was about to get worse.

Bonnie's expression turned sympathetic. "That's not good."

The woman would soon realize her own situation was far worse. "I can't stop to visit, because my grandpa just called and needs me right away."

Her grin grew wider. "Better get going then. John's not the kind of man to patiently wait."

"Please take care, Bonnie, and we'll get together soon enough, I'm sure."

She walked away without waiting for a response. Anxiety engulfed her, and she placed two fingers on her right temple to stave off the increasing pain. What she really needed was to head straight to bed.

Opal nodded briefly to Vicky Grisby coming from the opposite direction as she passed. For a middle-aged woman who'd been widowed too soon, she looked amazing. She had to be at least fifty, but with her toned body and cheeks pinkened by fresh air, she could easily pass for ten years younger. Maybe she and her daughter Candace were drinking from the same fountain of youth.

The second she thought that, she realized that Vicky would soon learn of her ex-son-in-law's death, too.

"Afternoon, Vicky." Bonnie's greeting cut across the distance, sounding stiff and unfriendly.

It seemed the negative energy from the dark moon was affecting everyone. She shouldn't stop to listen. Her headache demanded immediate attention, but she couldn't help wondering about the animosity between the two women.

Opal paused near the bath salts shop and surreptitiously glanced over her shoulder toward them.

An unapologetic sneer crossed Vicky's face. "Why do you bother talking to me when you know I can't stand you or your piece of trash son?"

Bonnie inhaled a shocked breath. "I never thought I'd hear those words from you, Vicky. You've been listening too much to your daughter, and you're only hearing one side of the story."

Oh, snap.

Opal shifted her gaze to the storefront. Apparently, the moms of the ex-spouses hadn't maintained their years-long friendship after their adult children had divorced.

"It's the only side that matters. Did you know that Beau doesn't have a pair of decent shoes because his so-called father doesn't pay child support? He's too busy spending money on his girlfriends."

Bonnie shook her head. "You know he's having a hard time with his business. I'm sure he's paying everything he can. He loves Beau."

Vicky snorted. "Pull your head out of the sand, Bonnie. Your son is a loser, and my daughter and grandson are paying the price. *They* are the victims in this situation."

Suffering distorted Bonnie's features. "Jason's a good boy, Vicky. He just needs to get back on his feet."

Vicky scoffed. "Whatever. When he mans-up and takes care of his responsibilities, then I'll believe that. Until then, he's trash to me."

Opal had heard enough and didn't want to end up in the middle of their dispute. She didn't look back as she hurried away from them, needing to get meds into her system before her headache fully developed.

It didn't sound like Vicky had anything good to say about Jason, and Opal couldn't help but wonder what had happened to the man since she'd left years ago.

He'd been the star of Crystal Cove, and now, he was dead.

Opal didn't stop until she reached her car. She dropped inside and rested her eyes for a few moments. When she opened them, lightning flashes distorted her vision. There was no help for her headache now but to sleep in a dark room. She started her car and drove straight past the police station toward home.

It was probably for the best anyway. The first words out of her mouth would have been a reprimand to her grandfather for not having notified the family already. Then that nastiness between Bonnie and Vicky would never have happened. Nor would she have had to make small talk with a woman who would soon be grieving.

From there, the argument between her and her grandfather would ensue, and she couldn't deal with that now. She'd had enough for one day. She needed her bed and the blessed relief sleep would bring.

Her headache pulsed as she parked in front of the classic Victorian cottage with cadet-blue plank siding and white shutters. The sight of it drew a small smile from her despite her headache. Home. She couldn't count the number of wonderful memories she and her grandfather had experienced there.

More than that, she couldn't wait to step into familiar surroundings, grab an ice pack, and fall into her soft bed.

Guilt pricked her when she fired off a message to her grandpa, letting him know her condition. She wasn't sure if he would understand, but she couldn't care at that moment. The police had the verbal version of her story, and it wasn't as though anything she did now would bring back Jason.

Her grandfather, the world, and everything else would have to wait until morning.

CHAPTER EIGHT

O pal woke with a start and found that morning had dawned. At first, she couldn't believe she'd slept for so long without waking, but then she remembered events from the previous day, and it made sense. A person could only take so much.

She lay perfectly still in bed, listening for what might have roused her, but the house seemed quiet. She glanced around her childhood bedroom, smiling at the colorful movie star posters and the trophies that she'd received from track meets in high school.

Her grandfather had raised her with love and happiness. So, why was he being a prickly sea urchin now? She couldn't imagine that she'd upset him by not letting him know she was coming home, but maybe that was it.

Honestly, she'd expected to be awakened by her grandfather's heavy fist pounding on her door, if not the previous night, then definitely that morning. But he'd left her alone.

Small mercies.

Perhaps he'd agreed her statement could wait, though he hadn't responded to her text message telling her so.

Either way, she needed to be up and at 'em.

She rolled from bed and sent gratitude to the heavens that her headache was gone, and she prayed her day would be much better than the previous one. She dressed, left her bedroom that had been an addition over the garage when her mother had been born, and she headed to the kitchen in search of food.

When she reached the bottom of the stairs, she paused to peek out the lace curtains to make sure her grandfather's car was indeed gone.

Sadly, she was relieved that it was.

Opal entered the kitchen and accepted the familiar surge of residual warmth, left by her grandmother and mother. Her grandfather had updated other parts of the house, but he'd left the sunny yellow kitchen and bright copper pots alone.

Perhaps he felt their presence there as well.

After a quick bite to eat, Opal left the house and headed to her car.

Her initial stop should be the police station, but she opted to go to the Rosewood Inn first. Perhaps if she secured a job before speaking to her grandfather, he'd be in a better mood.

She parked along the front of the inn, kissed the moonstone hanging from her neck for luck, and exited her car. She'd chosen the crystal in support of new beginnings. A new day. A new job.

Sun snuck through cracks in the clouds, giving the morning a fresh appearance. Things were definitely looking up.

The Rosewood Inn sat nestled between two hotels that towered over her. But the old lady, a transformed Queen Anne home from a different era, held her own. She'd been there longer than both buildings and looked much prettier to boot.

Flowering pink trees flanked the light-yellow two-story bed and breakfast. Dark green hedges surrounded gardens filled with white, lavender, and rose-colored hydrangeas that thrived in the cooler Pacific Northwest temperatures. Opal tried to imagine the town back in the day when the inn had been one of the few houses along the beach. Stunning then and still stunning now.

She climbed the stairs to the porch and reached for the worn black doorknob that might have been a remnant of the late-eighteenth century. The knob was stiff, and she had to force it to turn. Oddly enough, the heavy wooden door with frosted panes opened without a squeak.

She stepped into the rich wood-paneled room and inhaled the distinct scent of history. Three Bergère chairs upholstered in an old-fashioned floral print and a mahogany table held court in the center of the room, resting on a blue paisley rug. A plate of fresh chocolate chip cookies had been placed on the table, inviting guests to sit for a moment and enjoy a treat.

A rich mahogany counter with a speckled-brown granite top waited in a corner of the room, but no one was in attendance.

Opal studied an oil portrait of the first owner and his wife, while she waited for the hotel clerk to return. In the picture, Mr. Bourgeous boasted a round belly and thick moustache. Even though smiling was uncommon during that era, the serious look on the owner's face and something in his eyes chilled her.

On the other hand, Mrs. Bourgeous, also with a plump figure, radiated a delightful countenance. Opal expected that if they had been alive at the same time, she and Mrs. Bourgeous might have been friends.

Footsteps sounded on the steep staircase behind Opal, and she turned. A young, dark-haired couple near her age held hands as they descended. She smiled at the cute pair and guessed they were likely on their honeymoon, if their shiny new rings were a clue.

"Excuse me," the man said as they neared. "Do you work here?"

Opal shook her head. "No, sorry. I don't. I'm actually waiting for the hotel clerk, too."

The expressions on the couple's faces dropped. The man nodded in acknowledgement. "Okay, thanks. We're on our way to Oceanview to catch a live theatre performance, and we were looking for a dinner recommendation for afterward, but we need to be on the road right now, or we'll be late."

The woman glanced from her husband to Opal, and then leaned closer. "To be honest, the staff here are a little slow to respond."

Opal gave them a warm smile. "Oh, I might be able to help you. I do live in Crystal Cove, and I was here to apply for the open clerk position. I understand they've been shorthanded, which probably explains their inability to be on top of things. But the owner tries hard to run a good business."

The woman bit her bottom lip and wrinkled her nose in embarrassment. "Oh, sorry. Didn't mean to disparage her."

Opal held up a hand. "No, no. I'm sure Marla would be disappointed to know her guests weren't receiving topnotch service. I can recommend some fabulous restaurants if you tell me what you're in the mood for."

The man looked at his wife and shrugged. "I want fish. She wants a salad or hamburger."

Opal grinned. "I know the perfect place for you in Oceanview. Check out Bob's Tavern. Can't go wrong with the salmon or halibut, and his burgers are to-die-for. If you like beer, Bob carries several made by a local brewery located just outside town."

Pleased smiles lit their faces. "Sounds perfect," the woman said. "Thank you so much."

Opal returned their expressions. "My pleasure."

She watched them exit the hotel, happy she'd been able to help.

"You're hired."

Opal sucked in a surprised breath and turned. "Oh, my goodness. You startled me. I didn't hear you coming."

Marla Spencer stepped from the doorway that led into the backroom and brushed long strands of gray hair back from her face. A pink tinge colored her cheeks, and she seemed mildly winded. "Sorry that I wasn't here. The pilot light for a fireplace in one of the units across the street had gone out. Takes a minute to relight. But thanks for helping them and saying such nice things about our establishment. You're a gem."

Opal shrugged it off. "No problem. I meant what I said. I've loved the Rosewood Inn since I was a kid."

Marla nodded. "Same for me when I was growing up. Still love it now, but we both know maintaining old buildings isn't for the meek."

Yes, she did know that all too well from growing up in the Victorian cottage her grandfather owned. "True, but there's nothing like the unique charm of the old gals."

A sparkle lit in Marla's eyes. "Yes, yes. You understand. Hey, I meant it when I said you're hired. I heard you tell my guests that you were here looking, and you obviously have a way with people. If you want the job, it's yours."

Opal chuckled. "Wow. That was easy."

"Easy now. Might prove to frustrate you, though. Like I said, things don't always work as they should. You can use a computer, right?"

She snorted. "Of course."

The sound of a door slamming echoed from the floor above, and Opal raised her brows. "Trouble with guests?"

Marla waved away her concern. "Nah, it's likely our resident ghost. She likes to make herself known."

That snagged Opal's attention. Many owners of old buildings liked to boast about having a ghost, but she wasn't sure how many of them actually did. "Is this a real ghost or a tourist attraction?"

Her new boss winked. "Guess you'll find out soon enough. How soon can you start?"

Opal's pulse kicked up a notch. She hadn't been in town a day, and she already had a job. Her grandfather should be pleased. "Will tomorrow work? I just got back to Crystal Cove yesterday and need time to settle."

And deal with her grandfather.

Marla slapped the counter. "That works for me. Can you be here by nine?"

"That's perfect."

Warmth emanated from the kind woman. "And here I was thinking the day had started out crappy because we were shorthanded. You never know when the tide will turn, do you?"

Opal shook her head, wondering how many others had expected a different type of day than they'd received. Jason Conrad for sure. His mother, too. "You're right. You never know."

She headed outside, and oceanic winds teased her hair, blowing strands from her ponytail across her cheeks. She opted to leave her car this time and walk the several blocks to the police station. It wasn't far, and the fresh morning air would give her a chance to recharge before seeing her grandpa.

CHAPTER NINE

O pal neared the small white building with cedar shingles that had housed Crystal Cove's police department since she could remember. Fond memories washed away some of the apprehension forming in anticipation of seeing her grandfather.

She'd walked to the building from school nearly every day since she was five, up until she'd graduated from high school and moved across the country to complete the next phase of her witch training.

She had always hung out with Marcie Dorchester, the police chief's administrative assistant and part-time dispatcher for the department. The kind, older woman would pull up a chair for her, and Opal would steal a small space on the corner of her desk. She'd colored as a child and written dreaded English essays when she'd grown older.

Marcie was one of a handful of people that she'd missed most of all.

Eager to hug the older woman after being away for so long, Opal increased her pace. She carefully walked across the dilapidated parking lot, not certain why she avoided the spiderweb cracks, since she no longer had a mother and didn't have to worry about breaking her back.

But, still.

Opal climbed the wooden steps that led to the door of the police station, grabbed the rusted gold door knob and twisted it. She pushed inward, and the hinges squeaked with soothing familiarity.

Then she stopped short.

Instead of Marcie sitting behind the old metal desk, she found a younger woman, possibly late twenties, with a curtain of sleek, dark hair that reached down to her elbows. Her white blouse looked freshly pressed and her red lipstick recently applied. The name placard on the desk read Irina Fox.

The thought that Marcie might no longer work there caught Opal off guard and stole her words.

Ms. Fox's brilliant blue-eyed gaze traveled over Opal, leaving her feeling as if she had to defend her messy ponytail, worn hoodie, and ragged jeans. Her gaze settled on Opal's face with a look that chilled her soul. "May I help you?"

Opal was tempted to answer with a smart remark but found herself more concerned with what had happened to Marcie. "I'm here to see Chief Winston."

Irina's lips curved into one of the least-friendliest smiles Opal had ever encountered. "Do you have an appointment?"

Opal's hackles rose. She offered an over-the-top sweet smile. "I don't need one."

A glint of victory sparked in Irina's expression. "I'm sorry—"

"Opal?" Her grandfather's voice boomed from his office and cutoff his assistant.

Irina widened her eyes, looking surprised, and Opal responded by mimicking Irina's previous look of superiority before she stepped past the woman's desk toward him.

"Hi, Grandpa."

She made sure to emphasize "Grandpa".

John filled the doorframe of his office. "Glad you could make it."

As if she'd had a choice. "Sorry that I didn't come in last night."

He nodded in understanding. "I suppose that today is soon enough."

Opal cast a sideways look at Irina and then back to her grandpa. "Where's Marcie?"

John cleared his throat. "She retired."

Surprise rippled through her. "Retired? She's not much older than—"

Her grandpa held up a hand. "Don't say it."

The word, *you*, hovered on her tongue and then she swallowed it. "I never thought she would leave. Not until you did."

The police chief and his former assistant had begun their careers together and had complemented each other perfectly.

Opal narrowed her gaze. Something wasn't adding up. "Why?"

His bushy brows arched upward as though surprised she was questioning him. "Why?"

"Yeah. Why did she leave?"

Her grandpa flicked a glance in Irina's direction. The action took a split second, but Opal had caught it nonetheless. Irina was involved somehow, and Opal would discover what was behind those icy eyes.

John avoided her direct gaze and surveyed the office. "Many reasons, I suppose. A person doesn't want to work forever, you know."

Said the man who would hunt demons and vampires until his body wouldn't let him. Hopefully, she'd convinced him that witches weren't to be considered amongst that lot.

Irina focused her gaze on Opal and pasted on a fake smile that Opal saw right through. "She wasn't up to the work any longer. She made mistakes, and we couldn't trust her to keep information confidential."

We? Since when had Irina been part of the police department?

"Irina," John scolded. "Those are private personnel matters."

His assistant shrugged. "Everyone already knows it."

John turned to Opal. "We'll continue this conversation in my office."

She reluctantly followed her grandfather into his haven. He'd always seemed more at home in that space than at their actual house. He'd justified his workaholic attitude by declaring there were too many ghosts at home.

Not enough ghosts, if anyone were to ask her. She'd often dreamed of her mother and grandmother visiting her there, as the dead had sometimes been known to do to their kin, but she'd never been that lucky.

Opal supposed she would have understood his feelings better if she'd been old enough to remember her mother and grandmother. She recognized that void in her life, but it was hard to miss someone she'd never known.

He folded his impressive form into the worn leather chair that had occupied his office for as long as she could remember. A weighted sigh slipped from his chest as he studied her. "What happened to the crazy hair?"

She released an exasperated huff and sat opposite him. She shook her head in mock disappointment but still smiled. Black hair with purple streaks hadn't been *that* crazy in her estimation, but she knew his generation thought differently.

He lifted a brow, waiting for an answer.

She shrugged. "Got tired of it. Wanted a change."

John nodded with approval. "I like this color better anyway. Reminds me of your mama."

Opal smiled, even as a familiar ache echoed deep in her heart. "Thanks. I'll take that as a compliment."

"As you should."

Several seconds of silence passed, and the energy in the room shifted. She needed to get something off her chest. "I saw Bonnie Conrad yesterday."

Other than a small twitch of his eye, his expression remained the same, which stoked her irritation.

She narrowed her gaze, hoping to show him she was serious. "This was several hours...*hours* after I'd discovered Jason's body. How could you not notify her right away? Do you know how difficult it was to look her in the eye, knowing what I knew, and have a casual conversation as if her world hadn't collapsed? What if someone else had told her before you could? She was out on the street and vulnerable to that."

He didn't look the least bit ashamed. "Police procedure. I go by the book, and I trust my officers to follow protocol. First things first, Opal. I had a crime scene to control."

"What things are more important than his family?"

A hint of a smile curved his lips. He opened his mouth, and she knew the tirade that would follow. Her grandfather was never wrong.

She held up a hand before he could speak. "Never mind. I don't want to hear it. But I hope to the stars that you've told her by now."

He squared his shoulders and leaned back against his chair regarding her with watchful eyes. She knew that calculating look well enough to know she would never win an argument when he was in that mood.

"I know how to do my job, Opal. I've been doing it before you were a thought in your mother's mind."

She folded her arms and kept her mind as emotionless as the look on his face.

He paused for a moment, giving her enough time to continue the discussion. When she didn't respond, he slid a yellow legal pad across the desk until it rested in front of her. Then he dropped the nice pen Marcie had given him for his sixtieth birthday on top of it. "I need you to write an official statement. Everything you can think of. Everything you remember. Even the smallest detail."

She arched a brow, knowing if she spoke, she'd be pressing her luck. "Should I include how you sent me away like a child?"

He lowered his head and looked at her from beneath his brows. "Don't sass me. Just do what I asked."

She had to let this go for now. She didn't need an explosion between her and her grandfather the day after she returned. Instead of arguing, she relaxed her shoulders and picked up the pen "Of course."

She began to write but found she couldn't pretend certain things hadn't happened the day before. "I just wanted you to know the position you put me in with Bonnie yesterday and that you hurt my feelings when you sent me from the crime scene. I'm an adult, Grandpa. I can handle the sight of a dead body."

"Doesn't mean you should."

She wrestled with a way to talk to him so that he'd understand. "I'm not the same girl I was when I left. I've grown."

He stretched his arms straight out and then rested his hands on the back of his neck. "I guess time will tell if that's so. At least your hair has matured."

She wanted to tell him that her choice of hair color had nothing to do with maturity. Instead, she focused on her statement.

Her grandfather spent a few minutes typing on the computer, and then he stood.

She lifted her gaze. "Where are you going?"

"I need to speak with Irina and then drive over and talk to Ernie. He's always out on the river in the morning. Gets there mighty early. I hope he might have noticed something."

The idea of searching for clues sent her piqued her curiosity. "Can I ride along? I haven't seen you for years, and you've been busy since I've come home. I wouldn't mind some time together. Who knows? Maybe I'll be of help."

He snorted. "I don't need an over-enthusiastic wanna-be detective getting in the way of the investigation. Police work is serious business. You know this, Opal."

She swallowed the first retort that came to her lips in favor of keeping the peace. "I do know that, Grandpa. I'm not suggesting that I sleuth on the side. But, I may seriously consider following in your footsteps and join law enforcement."

Not exactly the truth. But, then again, not a lie. Following clues and discovering the real story greatly interested her.

John held her gaze for several long moments, his eyes dark and intense. Then he chuckled, and the verbal expression was a punch to her heart. "Good one, Opal. Good one. For a second there, you had me."

She gritted her teeth and worked to control her irritation. "I wasn't kidding."

He studied her with his famously perceptive gaze.

Opal hated that look. It usually followed with an interrogation and her confessing to whatever recent mischief she'd found.

Instead of glancing away, she held his gaze this time, trying to show him that she meant business.

The slow smile that curved his lips and highlighted the wrinkles around his eyes put her on guard. "Okay, then. I have a suggestion. Since you're so gung-ho to stick your nose in police work, you can intern at the police department this summer."

Excitement flared. "Work here?"

He narrowed his gaze. "*Intern*, I said. Volunteer. Not a paying job. Basically, you'd be a gopher for the department. Then you could get a good, healthy taste of what it means to be a cop. It's not at all glamorous like you seem to think."

She bristled. "For your information, stumbling across that body yesterday morning was anything but glamorous for me. Even so, I feel the need to find out what happened. If it was foul play, I'd like to see justice. Why is that a bad thing?"

Her grandpa nodded slowly in understanding. "It's not a bad thing. Admirable, in fact. But I think you have a skewed view of what police work is all about. Mostly, we handle domestic fights, auto accidents, and the occasional drunk person on the beach."

She shrugged. "It's still about making Crystal Cove a better place."

"Fair enough. Are you interested then? You still have to hold down a regular, paying job."

She could tell by the look in his eyes that he believed she'd turn him down. He was wrong. "Deal, and, just so you know, I've already secured employment at the Rosewood."

He paused and then conceded with a nod. "Okay then. We'll start with one of the more difficult parts of my job."

He gestured toward the door with a tilt of his head. "Ask Irina to come in here."

She stared at him dumbly. "Irina? What does she have to do with this?"

He folded his arms, leaned back in his chair, and released a big sigh. "She and Jason had an on-again, off-again relationship. Pretty sure they were in the off stage."

Her jaw slackened. "Even though she works here, she has no idea of what's happened? Is she aware someone died?"

John nodded. "She was out of town until late last night. With the police scanners yapping in the background this morning, it's likely she knows a person has died, but we don't share personal information on the radio, and she's smart enough not to ask me outright. She knows her place."

Meaning Opal didn't.

She ignored the jab.

"Ask her to come into my office," he repeated.

Opal stood, and her nerves tightened. This was one part of police work she wouldn't relish.

CHAPTER TEN

Opal peered into the quiet outer office and found Irina glancing between a document on her desk and her computer screen, while her fingers flew over the keys on the keyboard.

When the nasty woman didn't direct her gaze to her, Opal searched the air for an energy signature. At least she didn't detect any glaring animosity. Still, they'd both be happier if Opal had her way and never had to see Irina's face again.

Anxiety churned, and Opal cleared her throat.

Irina turned toward her.

"Could you come in here for a moment? The chief wants to speak to you."

A sliver of uncertainty crossed Irina's features, and Opal realized the woman wasn't as confident as she'd like everyone to believe.

Irina stood and walked toward her. Opal stepped back to allow her to enter the office. Both faced her grandfather's desk. Neither sat. Irina's uneasiness boiled over into her space, further igniting the same emotion inside her.

John glanced between them, and his wise eyes seemed to penetrate Opal's thoughts. "Take a seat."

She and Irina shared a quick glance before they claimed the two chairs in front of his desk.

He straightened and then leaned in. "First order of business. I will not tolerate my admin assistant and my granddaughter to be at odds in the station. You don't have to like each other, but this unpleasantness that seems to be brewing will cease. Understood?"

Opal swallowed a smart retort and nodded. She wanted to deny the accusation, but he was right.

"Yes, sir," Irina answered.

"Good. Next, Irina, when you get a moment, doesn't have to be done today, I want you to put Opal in the position of intern on our employee roster and take care of whatever that entails."

Irina sent Opal a look of irritated disbelief and then turned to the police chief. "We don't have an intern position."

If Opal didn't know what was looming on the poor admin assistant's horizon, she would have come back with a snarky remark, despite that she'd just promised to behave. Worse, she couldn't believe her grandfather would take care of petty housekeeping stuff when they had more important topics to discuss. Perhaps it really was time for him to retire, as Malcolm had suggested.

The chief fired a look of warning at Irina. "Make it happen."

Her shoulders slumped. "Yes, sir."

"She's a volunteer intern. No pay," he continued.

Irina straightened her posture and turned to Opal. Satisfaction gleamed in her eyes. "I'll need you to fill out the proper paperwork."

Opal shrugged, pretending the woman's gloating didn't bother her, pretending they weren't about to tell Irina of her ex-boyfriend's death. "Of course."

Irina stood.

The police chief held up a hand. "We're not finished yet."

His assistant managed to keep annoyance from her features as she sank back into her chair, but Opal sensed it rumbling beneath her calm surface.

When he had their full attention, he continued. "I know this is completely switching directions, and I apologize for that."

He exhaled a long breath and focused on Irina. "We have some bad news for you."

Her eyebrows shot upward, and the color drained from her face. "For me? Is she going to replace me?"

He shook his head gently and then turned to Opal. "I'll let you tell her. Keep it brief, and don't go into details."

Opal's blood iced over. *She had to tell Irina?*

Why in the world would he do such a thing? To punish her? To prove his point that police work could be difficult?

They both stared at her, waiting for her to speak, which didn't leave any time to puzzle through everything.

Her throat tightened, and she needed a moment to find her words.

Opal wished she hadn't previously met Irina, wished she didn't dislike her. She wanted to reach out and take Irina's hand as she delivered the news so that she could absorb some of the woman's grief. But that wasn't going to happen here.

She grounded herself with a breath. "Jason was found dead yesterday. He'd drowned."

Opal paused because she wasn't certain what details she could release, but it wouldn't have mattered if she'd wanted to continue because Irina's cry of disbelief would have buried them anyway.

Irina stood abruptly as tears welled in her eyes. "No. This can't be right. Jason is the one who died?"

John came around the side of the desk and put a comforting arm across her shoulders. "I'm so sorry. His body was found yesterday in the Chemawa River. Preliminary autopsy results suggest foul play might have been involved."

Opal widened her eyes. She knew it.

Irina pushed from him and vehemently shook her head. "That can't be."

A brief hint of compassion crossed her grandfather's face. "I'm sorry, Irina."

Opal opened her senses wide, searching for any kind of dishonesty or hidden emotions.

Tears that had mixed with Irina's black mascara trailed down her cheeks. She dabbed at her nose with the back of her shaking hand. "No, Chief. I can't believe this. I just...I can't."

From Opal's perspective, Irina's grief seemed genuine. She grabbed a handful of tissues from a box on a filing cabinet and pressed them into Irina's hand. "I'm so sorry."

Irina glanced at her as though she'd forgotten Opal was in the room. "Don't pretend you care about me."

Her words were like arrows. Opal shook her head, disagreeing. "I recognize we haven't started out on the best foot, but I wouldn't wish this upon anyone. You have my sincere sympathy."

With that, Irina cried harder, burying her face in the wad of tissues.

John gently helped her sit in the chair again and kneeled next to her. "Irina, I know this is incredibly difficult, but I have to ask you. Where were you the night before last, until noon yesterday?"

Irina's sharp intake of air knotted the nerves in Opal's stomach. "What are you saying? You think I caused this?"

The chief shook his head. "That's not what I'm saying at all."

The look in Irina's watery blue eyes sliced at Opal's heart, and she fought to erect the emotional wall that would protect her.

"But you think he was murdered," Irina said, her voice shaking. "You think I might be involved?"

Opal ached to put distance between herself and the poor woman next to her. She was sure her presence didn't help matters. Yet, she couldn't move.

John stood and returned to his seat across the desk. "You know I have to go by facts, and here is what I know. Jason drowned, and he was an excellent swimmer. These two things are in direct opposition to each other, making it unlikely he would have drowned if foul play or something medical wasn't involved."

He sighed, his age showing in his expression. "I see nothing to indicate you had any part in his death, if it wasn't accidental, but you also had a relationship with him. A relationship that was rocky at times."

She looked aghast. "How can you throw that in my face at a time like this? Couples fight."

Opal sensed her grandfather weakening his resolve, and she stepped in to help. "Irina, I know this is very hard, but the chief and his detectives will ask the same questions to everyone who knew him. He's not singling you out. He's probably trying to learn what he can so that he can mark you off the suspect list."

"Suspect list?" she whispered.

John nodded. "Let's get this business out of the way. Just tell me where you were. I know you'd asked for leave from work to spend time with your sister in Lincoln City. Is that what happened? If so, when did you return home?"

Terror invaded Irina's eyes. "I never went. I was going to, but then... But then..."

A heart-wrenching sob escaped her.

"But?" the chief pressed.

"But Jason asked me to stay, and we ended up in another argument that night."

Irina paused to inhale a shaky breath. "He left around ten, and that was the last time I saw him. Yesterday, I stayed home and avoided everyone and everything because it hurts to see others so happy."

The distraught woman buried her face in a wad of tissues.

Opal turned her gaze to her grandfather, but he didn't spare her a glance. Instead, he dragged a notepad toward him and jotted down notes. "Anyone there with you after he left?"

She lifted her tear-soaked gaze. "Just me. And my dog. But I swear I didn't do anything to hurt Jason. I promise. I—" Her voice broke. "I loved him."

The chief continued writing, his face an emotionless mask.

Again, an urge to reach out to Irina struck Opal, but she clamped down on her feelings.

John lifted his gaze. "Anything else to add?"

A sob escaped Irina, and she shook her head. "No. No. I just, I can't believe he's gone."

Something in her last words sounded hollow to Opal, and she focused more sharply on her senses as opposed to what her vision provided.

But the feeling, if it had meant anything, was gone, leaving nothing but grief in its wake.

Her grandfather stood and walked to Irina's side. "That's all the questions I have for you for now. Take some time off, okay? Take care of yourself. I'll get Hank's wife to fill in."

Irina sniffed and nodded. "Th-thank you."

"Can I give you a lift home?" he added. "Might be best if you weren't driving. I'm headed out anyway."

She looked at him with tear-stained eyes and then nodded.

He helped Irina out of her chair. "If you leave your keys, I'll have someone drop your car by your house in a while."

Irina allowed him to escort her out of his office. A moment later, the front door of the department opened, then closed, and she could only hear muted voices coming from down the hall.

Peace might have been nice after that horrendous meeting, except outrage on Irina's behalf filled her soul. Their conversation had flipped all over the place the moment Irina had entered his office. Opal had to wonder if her grandfather had done that on purpose to catch Irina in a moment of weakness to expose her guilt, if she had any.

Regardless, Opal felt like she'd been to Hades and back, too, even though the spotlight hadn't been on her.

Fuming, she grabbed the yellow legal pad she'd used earlier to begin her statement and wrote down everything she could remember about the crime. When she was done, she flipped the pad over and placed it on his chair where he wouldn't miss it.

She turned abruptly and smacked her knee against the corner of his desk. *"Son of a sea turtle."*

She needed to get out of there before she exploded. Needed fresh air. Needed the brisk breeze coming off the ocean to blow away the negativity she'd bathed in since arriving in Crystal Cove.

Opal emerged from her grandpa's office and stopped short when she found Lucas leaning over Irina's desk, writing something on a paper.

He glanced up. His gaze narrowed as he focused on her eyes. "What are you doing here?"

His question set her off, and anger poured out with her words. "My grandfather is the police chief. I don't need a reason to be here."

He lifted both hands in surrender. "Didn't mean to insinuate anything. Are you okay?"

The concern in his eyes exploited her emotions. No. She wasn't okay. Her grandfather had just been a first-class, insensitive jerk. "Are all police officers so brutal?"

He tilted his head to the side, and she sensed he was trying to understand her. "I typically don't trust anyone to be kind. Having said that, my first answer would be no, most officers, at least the ones around here, are not. They're just doing their jobs. Who are you referring to?"

Anxiety crawled beneath her skin, and she shot a glance at the door and freedom. "Never mind."

She strode past him and out the exit.

A slight breeze greeted her, caressing her face, but it wasn't enough. She needed the full force of the ocean's energy to blast her. Nothing else would do.

CHAPTER ELEVEN

Opal stepped off the cement boardwalk that separated the hotels from the ocean. Her flipflops sank into the soft, sandy beach, and she breathed easier. Unfortunately, the tide was out, so she had a fair distance to walk before she reached firmer sand and the blessed water.

Clouds had rolled in, chilling the air, while she'd been inside. She didn't care. The cooler temperatures would help calm the injustice raging inside her.

She hated to believe that her grandfather had been tougher with Irina because he wanted to prove to Opal that police work could be difficult. Yet, her gut told her that was exactly what had happened.

The fact that he'd gone through all that other nonsense of telling Irina to put Opal on the roster before he'd spilled the news, made her think he'd been trying to make them both as uncomfortable as possible.

He believed his own granddaughter was incapable of helping with police work, as if he knew her adult self. Then, the fact that he'd pushed his admin assistant, whom he should know well, made Opal wonder if Irina really might be guilty. Otherwise, why would he torture her so?

Opal's feet settled deeper with each step, and cool sand flooded her toes. The feeling of being home saturated her. She avoided the twigs and tiny bits of wood leftover from bonfires so they wouldn't jab the tender sides of her feet as she traversed the sand.

As much as she hated to cry, tears fueled by frustration swelled in her eyes. She quickly blinked them away. She shouldn't have to prove herself to her own grandpa. He should be on her side, regardless. Yes, he would likely think she needed training, but he could have been supportive instead of condescending.

Her friends in Sedona never would have treated her this way.

Too many bad things had happened since she'd arrived home, and her brain threatened to explode from trying to process the events. She'd need time to sort it all out.

"Enough," she whispered.

Opal wiped at the few tears that had spilled over and forged ahead. In the past, her grandfather's tactics to dissuade her might have worked, but she was a woman now. She'd come into her own powers.

When the debris in the sand lessened, she rolled up the hem of her jeans and kicked off her shoes. Her feet sank in the soft granules, and pure energy soaked through her. Immediately, her anxiety and anger eased like it always did when she came to the beach.

Ever since she'd been old enough to seek adventure by herself, she'd done this same thing, always finding solace from Mother Earth when she didn't have her own mother to comfort her.

When Opal reached the water-soaked, firm sand, she picked up the pace and strode straight toward the ocean, not stopping until water rushed over her toes. She shivered from the chill of it but knew her body would soon adjust to the temperature.

Energetic winds blew her hair about her face, and strands tickled her nose and cheeks. She exhaled a deep breath. The roar of the waves as they rushed toward shore drowned out all other sounds and the confusion circling in her brain.

If her grandfather couldn't accept and respect the value of her powers, then she would prove her worth to him by solving the murder using magic. She'd show him, and he'd have to listen then.

She had skills. They were strong, and she hoped someday to become formidable. No one could tell her that using her powers couldn't be just as effective as old-fashioned police work. She would figure this out.

She could kick herself for focusing more on her grandfather while he'd interrogated Irina. She should have paid closer attention to the subtleties and to Irina's reactions. She did remember, however, that Irina didn't have an alibi and that she and Jason's relationship had been rocky.

That was a start. Opal could dig and find out exactly how tumultuous it was. Folks in Crystal Cove were always willing to talk.

She would need to consider others, too.

Jason's ex-wife, for one. Rare was the divorced couple who could get along. Perhaps Jason and Kandace had tried to be amicable for the sake of their son, but Kandace was still a person of interest in Opal's book. She wondered how she might wrangle more information on potential suspects out of her grandfather at dinner that night. If she listened closely, she might also pick up information from others at the police station.

Either way, those were two great starting leads.

She smiled, proud that she'd concocted a course of action to help her with her endeavors. She *could* do this.

With her intentions set, Opal turned south and strolled parallel to the ocean. The clouds were spitting a misty rain, but not enough to deter her. Instead, she absorbed the glorious unseen, vibrant power that had always sustained her. Anyone could access it, not just witches. However, she was eager to try to harness it for later use, like Tara had taught her.

An unexpected surge of larger waves threatened to soak her jeans. She ran from the onslaught and laughed when she reached safety. She loved when the ocean wanted to play. Once the water had reached as far as it could, the waves tumbled over each other as they headed out to sea, and she drew close again.

In the distance, the entrance to the sea cave where she'd often sought solace and secretly played with her magic appeared as a dark spot at the base of a rocky hill. She remembered the treasures she'd buried there so many years ago when she and Penelope had played pirates.

Good times.

A sudden shift in energy stole her happy thoughts. She halted. Unwelcome prickles crept across her skin. Long before the witches had begun her training, her grandfather had always taught her to pay attention to her intuition.

She whirled around with a protective spell on her lips, and a surprised gasp escaped her instead.

Lucas strode toward her, and her senses tensed at the sight of him. What could the police department's second in command want with her now?

When he realized she'd caught sight of him, he smiled and lifted a hand in greeting, stealing her opportunity to leave without seeming rude.

His tall, imposing figure and the way he walked was already familiar to her. She didn't care to dig deep and know why. Instead, she offered a half-wave in return.

More intriguing than his physical looks was the aura around him. She'd never encountered anyone with one so dark who didn't carry a wave of equally dark emotion with him. She'd learned that was the best way to spot a troublemaker.

This man was different. He carried something dark, and she suddenly yearned to know why. If only she could sense his heart like she did with most others.

When he reached her, his expression grew serious. "Hey."

She lifted her chin in greeting. "Don't say bumping into me here was a coincidence. I won't believe you."

A brief hint of a smile teased his lips. "Too smart for that, huh?"

She cast him a wary look. "Should I be worried that the assistant chief of police is stalking me? Have I done something else wrong?"

She probably should have withheld the sarcasm.

He hooked a thumb into the front pocket of his pants. "Stalking? I hate that word. No, I'm not stalking you. After the way you left the station, I was concerned that you might not be all right."

Concerned.

His words surprised her, and she searched again for a pathway into his thoughts. "Okay, but why did you feel it was *your* responsibility to check on me? It's not like were friends. We're barely civil."

A shadow crossed his expression, and she worried she'd angered him. A ripple of emotion from him followed, and she realized the barb she'd tossed his way had struck a tender spot. The empath in her winced.

He held up a hand in truce and took a step back. "I apologize. I thought people in Crystal Cove looked out for one another. That's all I was doing. Didn't mean to overstep."

He turned to leave, and guilt kicked her in the gut.

She reached out a hand in his direction, surprised that she wanted him to stay. "I'm sorry. I'm not usually so rude."

With any other person, she wouldn't have rushed to judge. But this man was an enigma who left her on shaky ground. Not to mention, he'd cited her for speeding. Not the best way to start a friendship if that was what he was after.

When he met her gaze with a questioning one of his own, she released a heavy sigh. "It's not you. It's that I'm so frustrated with *that man.*"

"Your grandfather."

The fact that it was a statement as opposed to a question spoke volumes. "Yes. I know he loves me, but he seems determined to make my life as difficult as possible. If I didn't know better, I'd think he didn't want me to come home."

The look in Lucas's green eyes intensified. "Right. So, the fact that he mentions you every day doesn't mean anything."

His words stopped her. "He does? Every day?"

A hint of a smile hovered at the edge of his mouth. "Opal makes the best chocolate cake. Opal has her mother's eyes. Opal runs an eight-minute mile. I know you better than you'd probably like."

Embarrassment heated her cheeks. "Ten-minute mile. Lost some speed after...an injury."

She wasn't about to mention the cruel hex she'd endured.

He chuckled. "I stand corrected."

Maybe she was looking at Lucas all wrong. Perhaps this man who'd worked closely with her grandfather for the past few years could shed some insight on what had happened while she'd been gone. "If he's so proud of me, then why does he refuse to see me as an adult? I could help him if he'd just let me."

An odd shiver raced over her, and she stopped speaking before giving away too many details of how she'd like to help. She couldn't be sure, but it seemed his eyes had darkened, and dare she say, beguiled her? Something had rendered her comfortable enough that she'd almost talked about her craft and abilities.

She blinked, and his irises appeared green once again.

He shrugged. "I can't imagine he wouldn't like help. He does have Eleanor cleaning house and looking after him, but..."

As much as she didn't particularly care for Eleanor, she had to appreciate her services, which had allowed Opal to leave for Arizona without feeling like she'd abandoned her grandpa.

Opal wanted to explain that what she meant was she'd like to help with police work if possible, but she doubted Lucas would be any keener to it than her grandfather.

Not only that, but she couldn't get past the small warning intuition tossed her way, telling her to be careful with Lucas. "In his eyes, I'm still a kid. That's how he's treating me."

Lucas cast a quick glance over her. "You're definitely not a kid."

He coughed then, as though he'd realized his reply might be construed as flirtation, which she did wonder if that had been his intention.

He shifted his stance and glanced toward the boardwalk. "I'd guess a lot of parents and grandparents don't want their kids to grow up. Especially ones who've seen what he's seen in life."

Opal tilted her head and studied him, curious if he was alluding to her grandfather's relentless pursuit of paranormal persons or not. If so, she wondered if Lucas shared the same disturbing beliefs on the matter. "Maybe so."

For all she knew, he could be a paranormal hunter, too. Maybe that's why her grandpa had hired him. Maybe that's why she'd sensed that her grandpa didn't want her home and why she'd sensed something dark about Lucas. Perhaps he was a danger to her.

She stared at him for a long moment, wondering how much she trusted him with her thoughts. "I have some questions for you, if you don't mind."

"Shoot."

"If you're the assistant police chief, why are you doing mundane traffic stops? Why didn't my grandfather promote Hank instead? He has more seniority. And why did he order you to collect the evidence I'd found instead of someone with less authority? He treats you like you're a rookie."

Lucas snorted. "So many questions."

Overzealous embarrassment heated her cheeks, and she shrugged to downplay it. "I'll admit I'm curious about a lot of things."

He accepted her statement with a nod. "Let's just say your grandfather is a complicated fellow."

She waited for him to impart something more. When he didn't, she raised her brows. "That's it? That's all you're going to say?"

She knew she was closer to finding out the reason he'd been hired, but he didn't seem inclined to share more.

Instead, he twisted his lips into a knowing grin, giving her a glimpse of an actual smile. "Hank's not far from retirement, just like your grandfather. The police chief and I are a good team. We balance out each other. Each with our own strengths."

"And weaknesses?" she couldn't help but ask.

A glint sparked in his eye. "We all have them."

Was he suggesting he knew hers? The thought left her unsettled. "I suppose we do."

Then again, if he was a paranormal hunter and could read her thoughts, they wouldn't likely be having this conversation.

Would they?

He tilted his head toward the boardwalk. "Now that I see you're okay, I'll let you get back to your day."

Opal flicked a glance toward the sea cave and decided she'd have to come back to it another time. She wasn't ready to let Lucas go just yet. Not when he might be a good source of information. "Is it okay if I walk back with you? I have stuff I need to do."

He seemed pleased by the idea. "Sure. If you don't mind walking with a stalker."

CHAPTER TWELVE

Opal fell in step beside Lucas as they traced their paths back across the beach. She had to walk faster than normal to keep up with his lengthy stride, and she filled her lungs with the fresh sea air to compensate for her exertion.

She slid a sideways glance toward him, glad that he no longer wore his hat, which allowed her to see his eyes better. "I'm curious what you think about Jason Conrad's death."

The familiar hint of a smile crossed his lips. "You want me to discuss police business with you?"

Renewed agitation churned. "It's not like I don't already know things. I was the one who'd found the body."

He nodded thoughtfully. "So, I'd heard. That was part of the reason I was concerned about your state of mind when you stormed out of the police station."

His description of her actions embarrassed her. "I didn't storm."

He caught her with a look that argued otherwise.

Unfortunately, he was right. She was beginning to discover he had a good radar for detecting half-truths. "I was angry. Okay?"

He shrugged. "I don't doubt it. You had a rather rough welcome home yesterday."

She snorted. "Yes, and honestly, you contributed to it."

That grin again. "The ticket?"

"You could have let me go."

"You could have not gone over the speed limit in the first place."

She hated the way he turned that back on her. Not to mention, they'd gone significantly off track from what she'd intended to discuss.

She blew out a frustrated breath. "Let's forget that. What I really want to know is if you think Jason was murdered. My grandpa said initial autopsy results suggested he might have been."

So much for subtle questioning.

Clouds covered the sun, and he stopped and turned to face her. "That's an interesting question. Is that what you believe?"

The intensity in his eyes made her wonder if she was on to something. She shrugged, trying not to act excited. "Jason was an excellent swimmer when I knew him. If he'd been in the ocean and a riptide had caught him unaware, then maybe I'd believe he'd drowned. Maybe. But swimming in the Chemawa?"

She shook her head. "I sense foul play."

He nodded thoughtfully.

She widened her eyes in expectation. "You're not going to tell me anything?"

He slowly shook his head, even as a smile teased his lips. "I'm sorry, Miss Mayland. That would be against policy."

Fine. She'd have to try an alternate way into his thoughts. She hoped her next question wouldn't be a huge mistake. "My grandpa mentioned sirens. I'm curious if you believe in them or if we've had some visit the area."

His eyes darkened ever so slightly and set her on edge. "Sirens, huh? No, the police chief has not shared that suspicion with me."

After a moment, he added, "But I expect, if that's the case, he will."

The thought of sirens being an actuality sent goosebumps to her skin. "Does that mean we've had some visit Crystal Cove? Never happened the whole time I was growing up."

He shrugged. "Not that I'm aware of."

But he hadn't said no, which meant...

Perhaps things had changed. If so, her grandfather would likely shoot them as ask questions. She hoped that wouldn't happen because she'd love to talk to one. "Then it's a possibility? Could one of them be guilty?"

Which would mean she had other suspects to add to her currently small list.

A placating smile crossed that darned mouth once again. "Sorry, ma'am. I really can't discuss case details with you."

She sighed with exasperation. "Fine. I'm sorry I bothered you."

She turned from him. Their whole conversation had been a waste of time. She would have been better off keeping her eyes on the ocean for signs of sirens instead of his interminable, ever-changing eyes.

Opal managed several long strides before he caught up with her. It surprised her that he took the trouble.

"Look, you need to understand that talking about a case could jeopardize and possibly cost me my job."

She refused to look at him. "I come from a law enforcement family. I get it."

They walked for several minutes in silence before her irritation dissolved back into eagerness to know more. She might despise herself for her weakness, but there was no way around it. "Can you tell me what you think about Irina, then?"

He chuckled, and she caught a glimmer of light in his eyes. "Do I think she killed him?"

"No," she corrected. "I'm not asking about the case. I'm asking what you think of her as a person. I'd like to know the people my grandfather has in his life."

He raised his brows. "Like me?"

His poignant question hit home. Exactly like him. But she'd have to let that go for now. "Perhaps, but I'm asking about Irina. Is she a good person?"

He seemed to ponder her question for a moment. "I'd say she is. She's a great admin assistant. Keeps us all organized and in line."

Opal rolled her eyes. "Except she stole Marcie's job."

He agreed with several nods. "I was sad to see Marcie go, too. She's a great lady."

For the first time since she'd met Lucas, she found something to like about him. "Do you know her well?"

He nodded. "I've been going to her house every Tuesday night for dinner. She likes the company, and you can't beat her cooking. Except she's been out of town for the past couple of weeks, and man, have I missed her."

The jealousy bug gnawed into Opal's heart, and she frowned. "*I* used to go to her house every Tuesday night for dinner, back before I left for school."

"Hmm..." he said but didn't comment further, as though he was certain he could maintain his position as the Tuesday night guest even though Opal had returned.

She was sad to learn she'd have to wait longer to see her old friend. "How long will Marcie be gone?"

"She's visiting her kids in Washington. Said she'd come home when she was ready. I'll let you know when I hear from her."

When *he* hears from her? Had he usurped her as Marcie's unofficially adopted child?

Just like that, they were at odds again. She didn't know how to fix it, or if she even wanted to. Really, all she needed from Lucas was information.

The lack of sunshine and her sweater now damp from the rain left her chilly, and she wrapped her arms about her. "So, Irina's a good employee. What about outside of work?"

He chuckled. "You'd make a great interrogator, you know?"

"That's not a bad thing," she countered, still bristling from her grandpa's comments.

"Not at all," he agreed.

He shrugged out of his jacket, and before she realized his intent, he settled it about her shoulders. Warmth enveloped her, and his concern touched her heart more than she liked. "Thank you, but it's not necessary."

"The lady is cold," he answered, leaving no room for argument.

As much as she wanted to refuse his generosity to spite him, the chill in her bones wouldn't let her.

Instead, she decided she'd use it to her advantage. If she had his jacket, she could hold it hostage for more information.

She slipped her arms into the sleeves and then tilted her gaze upward to his face. "Okay, if you won't tell me more about Irina, then what about Jason's ex-wife?"

He lifted both brows. "Kandace?"

She frowned. "You say that like he has more than one."

He chuckled. "No, just the one. Yeah, I suppose if we thought he'd been murdered, she would be a suspect."

They reached the end of the beach, and he held out his hand to help her up the large step to the sidewalk. Not wanting a repeat of their earlier odd interaction, she pretended she didn't notice and stepped up unassisted.

He dropped his hand as if he hadn't offered it, and they strode toward Main Street, which would lead to her car.

Time was ticking. "Does that mean you don't think Jason was murdered?"

"I didn't say we'd ruled out murder."

Seriously? He took vague answers to a new level.

She threw her hands up and growled out her frustration. "You know, I can visit Kandace myself and get a feel for her emotions, see if she's acting shifty. I don't *need* you to tell me anything."

He lifted his chin in acknowledgement. "Good to hear. Just so you know, I wouldn't try to stop you."

Was he encouraging her then? The man made no sense. "You're worse than my grandfather."

He stopped at First Avenue and faced her. She was about to ask why he'd halted, but she caught sight of his SUV not far down the block.

A teasing light entered his eyes. "If you're referring to his work ethic, I'll take that as a compliment."

Annoyance bubbled inside her. "I was referring to his stubbornness."

Her comment didn't dent his expression in the slightest, and he gestured toward his car. "I'm just over here. Why don't you let me drive you back to the station?"

She narrowed her gaze, not mentioning that her car wasn't at the station. Last chance. "Will you tell me what I want to know?"

He grinned. "Probably not."

She lifted her nose in distaste. "Then I'd prefer to walk."

They stared each other down for a long moment, and he caved with a nod. "Have it your way. Good afternoon, Ms. Mayland."

Barely veiled exasperation reared its head again. "Later."

She turned and strode away.

The man drove her insane.

What she really needed was to avoid him altogether. She didn't need his help to solve this case. She had her own set of tools that would help her. Ones that, at the very least, he wouldn't understand. At the worst, he might try to make her disappear.

For now, she'd take a drive to see how much Crystal Cove had changed since she'd been gone. She'd stop by her best friend Penelope's house to see if she was at home. They never lacked for things to talk about. She probably should visit her mama and grandma at the cemetery, but she wasn't sure she was up to that quite yet.

At dinner, she'd let her grandfather know exactly what she thought of his interrogation efforts and see if she could squeeze further information from him.

Tomorrow, she'd pay a visit to Bonnie to offer her condolences on the loss of her son. She wished she dared to do the same with Kandace like she'd told Lucas she would, but the fact was she didn't know Jason's ex-wife all that well. She'd have to watch for a different opportunity instead.

CHAPTER THIRTEEN

Muted rays of sun peeked between clouds and hung low in the sky when Opal finally pulled into the gravel drive of her childhood home. No one had answered Penelope's door, so she'd save her surprise visit for the following day. And not much had changed in town either, but her time spent casually driving along the coast with its familiar curves and stunning ocean views had been perfect.

Her grandpa's police cruiser sat parked nearest to the house, while a sporty white Cadillac cozied up next to it. Opal exhaled and worked to keep her annoyance at bay. Penelope had warned her that Eleanor and her grandfather often ate dinner together, so Opal had to assume the Cadillac was hers and that they would have a dinner guest.

Which meant she wouldn't have time alone with her grandfather.

Opal wished she could make herself like her more. They had a personality clash or something. Opal often wondered if she'd subconsciously connected the absence of her mother and grandmother to the appearance of Eleanor and that was why she didn't like her.

Who knew?

Opal stepped onto the porch and pushed open the door. Soft laughter emanated from the kitchen and curiosity drew her toward the sound. She'd expected to find two smiling faces, not her grandpa standing inches from Eleanor with a stupid look on his face.

Her grandpa shot a look in Opal's direction, and his eyes widened in surprise. He pushed away from Eleanor causing her to stumble backward. Eleanor gasped and caught the edge of the table to keep from falling over.

Both looked guiltier than sin, and Opal narrowed her gaze in response.

"Oh, hey." His voice sounded breathy, and she did not want to know why.

Eleanor drew the edges of her blouse together across her neck, and a deep blush pinkened her cheeks. "We didn't hear you come in."

No kidding.

Opal lifted a hand in awkward greeting. "Hi. Uh, sorry. I'll try to make more noise next time."

Her grandfather coughed to cover his obvious embarrassment, and Eleanor hustled to the stove. He took a seat at the table, and she lifted a wooden spoon lying next to a big pot and stirred. Whatever she had cooking smelled divine.

"Beef stew?" Opal guessed.

Eleanor sent her a quick glance, obviously grateful for the change in subject. "Yes. It should be ready. John said you'd likely be here for dinner."

Though a flush still hovered on her grandpa's cheeks, he dared another look in Opal's direction and then frowned. "What's that?"

She returned his expression, not understanding.

He pointed toward her chest. "What are you wearing?"

Opal glanced down and then froze. Lucas's jacket still covered her in a warm hug. "Oh..."

She was sure her countenance turned far brighter than her grandfather's face had, and she quickly shrugged out of the offending item. She tossed the jacket on a stool sitting near the wall and stepped away from it. "It's a long story. Just one of your men being a gentleman, offering me his jacket because I forgot mine."

John narrowed his gaze. "Lucas."

His words came out like a condemnation that left her brain scrambling.

"Yes," she said defensively and took a seat at the table. "I was at the beach, and it turned cloudy. I hadn't thought to bring a jacket."

"You were walking on the beach together?"

Eleanor chuckled. "Sounds romantic."

John shook his head. "You're back in town for only a day, and already the guys are coming 'round."

Opal shot Eleanor a sideways glance. "Not romantic."

She shifted her annoyed gaze to her grandpa. "And there were no guys *coming 'round*. He offered me a jacket because it was cold and rainy. End of story."

And she'd sure appreciated its warmth throughout the day. But she hadn't wanted to go home to get her own or to see Lucas again so soon to return it to him.

John leaned back and locked his fingers behind his head. A half-smile tilted his lips. His stance might have appeared casual, but Opal recognized the brutal interrogator she'd witnessed earlier in the day. "The question is, why were you on the beach together?"

She huffed. "We weren't. I was. Then I ran into him. Or he ran into me."

"Which was it?" her grandfather asked.

The older couple's watchful gazes heated the room at least ten degrees, and Opal struggled to keep her story clear. "I was walking, and he approached me."

The police chief's gaze remained steady. "Why?"

She threw her hands into the air in a show of frustration. "How would I know? You'd have to ask him."

John nodded. "I will."

Oh, no. *No, no, no, no, no.* That would make things a hundred times worse. "No, you won't."

He lifted a defiant brow, challenging her statement. "Of course, I will. It's my job to know if my officers get out of line."

She stared at him for a long moment, and then finally realized the only way to prevent a social train wreck was to speak the truth. "Fine. I'll tell you why he was on the beach."

A sly smile crossed her grandfather's lips, and he leaned forward. "Let's hear it."

He could give her that smug smile all he wanted. It wouldn't last long. "Officer Keller was in the office when I left."

John gave a curt nod. "Yeah, I saw him when I took Irina home."

Resurrected anger pulsed inside Opal. "Irina was a hot mess, and it was all because you were so awful to her."

He squared his shoulders. "Irina had just learned her former boyfriend had died. How would you expect her to act?"

Opal wouldn't let him talk his way out of this one. "Of course, she would be upset. But you were cruel to her, launching straight into an interrogation after telling her Jason was dead."

"Best time to question someone is when they're off balance."

Unfortunately, her words didn't affect him in the least, which made her angrier. "You didn't just question her. You practically accused her of doing it."

Eleanor gasped. "John. You didn't."

He glanced between the two women and then stood. "I won't be questioned on my choices. You aren't officers of the law, and you haven't been trained in interrogation tactics. Don't presume to tell me how to do my job."

Eleanor sighed her disapproval and turned back to the stew.

With one opponent down, John fixed a challenging look at Opal. "None of this explains why you were on the beach with Lucas."

He thought he could switch to offensive tactics, and she'd back down. Which, of course, she had no intention of doing. "I went to the beach to cleanse my soul after watching you with Irina. I know you were harder on her because I was there, because you wanted to show me in callous terms how difficult it can be to be a police officer. Don't try to deny it."

He didn't.

She inhaled a deep breath. "Do you know how that made me feel knowing she suffered unnecessarily because I was there?"

He blinked slowly and shook his head. "It's all part of the job, Opal. If you want to be involved in police work, you'd better toughen up."

She stood, too. She'd endured enough for one day. "You know what? I've got to go. I forgot I told Penelope that I'd meet her tonight. If there's any stew left, Eleanor, please save some for me. I'll do the dishes when I get home."

She took a step. Turned and snatched Lucas's jacket from the stool and strode from the room. Taking it with her might have appeared incriminating, but at that point, she didn't care.

Her grandfather had already judged and condemned her. If she had known this would be her homecoming, she wasn't certain she would have returned to Crystal Cove.

CHAPTER FOURTEEN

Far too many negative emotions swirled in Opal's head as she opened the car door and fell inside. Once she had it shut, she released a loud growl of frustration.

She slipped the phone from her pocket and dialed Penelope's number. So much for showing up unannounced and surprising her friend. She'd have to settle for hearing Penelope's surprised voice when she told her she was home.

Penelope answered on the first ring, sounding excited. "Opal? Tell me my predictions are correct, and you're back in town."

Just like that, Opal's anger dissipated. "As a matter of fact, I am, and I'd love some girl time. It's been a rough couple of days."

"Meet me at Finnegan's?"

Opal laughed. "I'm already in my car."

Five minutes later, Opal pulled into the small parking lot next to Crystal Cove's favorite watering hole. She parked and stepped from her car, glancing toward the nearby Chemawa River that passed through town. The same river where she'd found Jason.

Night had fallen, and most of the shops had closed for the day. Several tourists walked the street, many of the couples walking hand in hand. A hush hovered in the air, and Opal could breathe again.

She pulled open the heavy wooden door that led into Finnegan's, and a wild Irish jig greeted her. Finn O'Brien's Irish pub wasn't huge and could get crowded on weekends when a larger number of tourists flocked to the area. Luckily, the gathering was sparse tonight.

Opal immediately located her friend at a table near the bar and headed in that direction. Penelope's hair was short and darker, but she still wore the same periwinkle hoodie she'd favored forever.

She widened her eyes when she spotted Opal and jumped up from her seat. The moment they were within arm's reach, Penelope wrapped her with a fierce hug.

Her friend blinked rapidly as she gave Opal the once-over.

Opal chuckled, holding back her own feelings. She realized now just how much she'd missed her bestie.

Emotion spilled from her and touched Opal.

"You're not going to cry, are you?" Opal asked.

Penelope sniffed, linked her arm through hers, and headed toward the table where she'd been sitting. "I might. Six years is a long time to be apart."

They slid into the booth on opposite sides of the table. Opal's smile blossomed from her heart to her face. "I didn't realize how long until I came back. It's so amazing to see you. Tell me everything."

A mischievous grin played on her lips. "Let's see. My cousin Carole Anne moved to town."

Opal hadn't seen Carole Anne since she was sixteen, but she adored the crazy, warm-hearted girl. "I love Carole Anne."

Penelope snorted and tilted her head from side to side. "I do, too, but having someone constantly around with so many wild ideas has the tendency to cause mayhem. Her four-year-old twin boys act exactly the same."

That news surprised Opal. "She has kids? And a husband?"

Penelope quickly shook her head. "She's not married. Whoever the father is, we don't talk about him, either. She just showed up one day with a protruding belly and that was that."

A secret that sounded awfully close to her own circumstances. Opal had never known her father, and no one, including the townsfolk, seemed to know anything about him, either.

The urge to know the truth was already under Opal's skin. "How can you stand not knowing what happened?"

"Well, I have my suspicions. But nothing I've been able to confirm."

Intrigued, Opal leaned forward. "What kind of suspicions?"

Penelope glanced around to ensure no one was within hearing distance. "I think a werewolf is the father."

Opal widened her eyes in surprise. "A werewolf? No way," she whispered.

What if her own father was a werewolf?

Her friend nodded. "You should hear those two boys when they cry."

Opal realized it was a joke, and she laughed. "Good one. You had me believing."

Penelope shook her head. "No, seriously. I had this vision of a man with long dark hair kissing Carole Anne. The next moment, his eyes turned yellow, he howled and ran off."

She wasn't sure what disturbed her more, the vision or the fact that Penelope had one. "Vision?"

Penelope reached across the table and gripped Opal's hand. "I told you a while back in an email that I'm a psychic."

Opal snorted. She'd wondered if Penelope had *found* her psychic abilities because she'd always yearned to have something cool like Opal's gifts and witch ancestors, or if she'd spoken the truth. "Yeah, but I didn't think you were serious."

Her friend frowned.

Opal sent her an apologetic smile and then filtered the idea through her memories looking for signs. "Really?"

Penelope nodded. "Apparently, it's been in my family for ages, but no one talked about it since it's such a sketchy thing these days."

She studied her friend's aura more closely. "Okay, maybe I can see it now. You do have purple outlining your aura. And there was that time when my dog ran away. I was going to call you to help me look for him, but the next second, you rang the doorbell saying you knew I needed you."

Penelope grinned. "And the time when I predicted Steven was going to ask you to prom."

Opal snorted. "No, that one you found out because you saw a text on Gary's phone that Steven had sent."

Her friend dissolved into bubbly laughter. "Okay, you're right on that one. I'd forgotten about the text. But it was my psychic powers that told me you needed me. That night and tonight."

Opal narrowed her gaze. "Tonight, too?"

She nodded. "I mean I did question that knowledge because I thought you were still in Sedona. But here you are."

Opal made room in her thoughts for the idea that it might be true. "Psychic. Wow. That's incredible."

Penelope seemed pleased with her ability. "It is pretty amazing."

Opal stared into her friend's crystal blue eyes. "Okay. Tell me something you can see about me."

Penelope opened her palms upward and rested them on the table. She closed her eyes and took a deep breath.

Several awkward seconds passed before she spoke. "I see a tall, dark-haired stranger coming into your life, but he seems to like to hide in the shadows."

Opal snorted, and Penelope opened her eyes. "Isn't that what all psychics tell women?" Opal asked.

Disappointment flitted across Penelope's features. "Laugh now, but I'm serious. This will happen."

She shook off her doubt and smiled. "Okay. I trust you. What else do you see?"

"It's dark out. A sleek black cat is following you, and you're wearing a fancy black dress with sparkles."

Opal folded her arms and tried to imagine a scenario where that might actually happen. "You know I'm not a fancy-dress kind of girl."

Penelope focused a sharp gaze on her. "It helps if you believe in me. Gives me extra insight or power. Something."

Opal agreed with a nod and exhaled. "I believe you. I do. Could this cat be my familiar?"

"I'm not sure."

Most other witches had a familiar of some sort, but she'd never been lucky enough to find hers. It seemed discovering her familiar was a lot like finding her soulmate. Neither seemed to be on the horizon.

Though she did adore kitties, and a sleek black cat sounded fun.

Her friend opened her hands palms up again and closed her eyes. Confidence radiated from her this time. "Finn is on his way to our table and will be here within seconds."

Opal's jaw slackened as the fifty-year-old owner of the pub strode straight toward them.

"Good Gaia," Opal whispered.

Finn looked much the same as before, though he now had gray at his temples and threaded through his chestnut hair. Still, she was sure the green-eyed bachelor with a charming smile had no problem attracting plenty of ladies.

Penelope opened her eyes just as Finn arrived.

He flashed them a set of perfect white teeth and placed bar napkins on the table. "Hey ladies. Looking good. Glad to see you back, Opal. What can I get you?"

"I'll have the Coastal Haze beer," Penelope said and then glanced to Opal.

"Just ice water for me."

"You got it."

After Finn disappeared with their orders, Opal frowned. "I really need something to take off the edge before I head home again, but I'm driving."

Penelope sighed. "Staying with your grandpa isn't what you'd hoped?"

Opal narrowed her gaze. "Are you asking me or telling me?"

Her friend laughed. "I sense a disturbance circling you, but I'm not sure if it's your grandpa or something else."

Could be a million things after the two days she'd had. "I thought it would be awesome coming home, but I'm afraid Eleanor practically lives at my house, and my grandpa is being a stubborn jerk."

Penelope sent her a commiserating smile. "I told you there was a little something-something going on between those two."

Unfortunately. "I know, but I didn't exactly believe it until I saw them. Pretty sure they'd been making out right before I walked into the house."

Penelope winced. "Oh. Awkward."

"Right? Not something I want to see. And then my grandpa started in on me, and I couldn't stay and eat dinner with them after that, or I'd likely strangle him. Can you picture the headlines? Crazy witch kills her police chief grandfather with bare hands."

Penelope laughed and then accidentally snorted, a trait Opal found endearing but Penelope despised. Her friend covered her mouth in embarrassment before glancing around the room. "Don't make me laugh like that."

Opal grinned. "Sorry."

"Why is your grandpa being such a butt?"

She waited for Finn to deposit their drinks and leave before she responded. "I'll tell you, but you have to let me finish before you laugh."

Penelope nodded to give her the go-ahead.

"I had this awesome idea to come back to Crystal Cove and help my grandfather. I feel like the police department could use a person like me."

Penelope leaned in conspiratorially. "I'd wondered if they could use a psychic, too, but I didn't dare ask."

Opal sighed. "Unfortunately, he can't see the value in using someone like us. Drives me crazy that he won't listen."

Penelope sipped her drink and then chuckled. "That's family for you."

Frustration rattled inside Opal. "So...I've been entertaining the idea of trying to solve Jason's murder and prove him wrong. Then maybe my grandpa could see."

Penelope exhaled and placed a hand against her chest. "Yeah, I'd heard about Jason. Hard to keep that a secret."

Opal nodded. "I'm the one who found him. Add that to the list of awesome things that have happened since coming home."

Then guilt slammed her. "Sweet Gaia. I shouldn't complain. At least I'm alive."

Penelope nodded solemnly and whispered. "I hadn't heard anyone mention murder though. You think someone killed him?"

She eyed her friend closer. "I do."

An idea formed in Opal's mind. "I don't suppose your abilities are giving you any clues?"

Her friend's expression dropped. "Honestly, I think I'm only half-psychic. Maybe a quarter. Sometimes I'm positive I'm right, like with the father of Carole Anne's children. Then other times, things are kind of blurry."

Opal didn't agree with Penelope's assessment of her skills. "I think a person is either psychic or not. Maybe you need to use your perception more to get better at it, like with me and my spells."

Penelope took a drink, studying Opal over the rim of her glass as she did. She set the glass down. "Maybe so. Either way, I believe in you, and you know I'd be happy to try to help you whenever you need it."

Her idea made complete sense. Even if Penelope wasn't truly psychic, she could help in plenty of ways such as another set of eyes and ears on the town. "That is a fabulous idea."

Penelope's aura brightened, and the charming smile returned to her face. "I would love that so much. We can poke around quietly, but I bet we can discover what really happened."

Opal nodded as the idea cemented in her head. "Yes. That's exactly what we'll do. Thank the stars that I can always count on you to have my back."

CHAPTER FIFTEEN

As much as Opal had relished the idea of sleeping in now that she was back in her own bed, the noises in the house had brought her fully awake by six a.m. She'd kept to the bathroom and her bedroom until eight, not wanting to face her grandfather and all the negativity that seemed to come with him lately. She swore he hadn't been so grumpy when she was growing up, but perhaps her view of him from a child to an adult was what had changed.

When the house seemed quiet, Opal slipped from her room and tiptoed into the thankfully empty kitchen. She poured a travel mug of coffee, folded two slices of toast laden with butter and raspberry jam in a paper towel and hurried out the door. No sense hanging about, waiting for someone to ruin what would likely be a hard day anyway.

She eyed Eleanor's Cadillac as she strode past and wondered if she had gone home or stayed the night, wondered if she was in the house somewhere, cleaning, or still lounging in bed. Then Opal decided she really didn't want to know.

A few minutes later, she parked on a dead-end road and listened to the roar of the ocean while she ate her breakfast in peace. Afterward, she had a good forty minutes before her first day at work, as she'd planned. She drove three blocks and parked in front of Bonnie Conrad's gray-washed, cedar-shingled two-bedroom home where the woman had raised her two children.

Opal mentally prepared herself for the grief she'd encounter and then opened her car door. Bonnie had always been awake with the sunrise, so Opal wasn't worried about the time. What did concern her was Bonnie's reaction now that she knew Opal had been the one to find him and that Opal hadn't said anything when she'd encountered her the previous day.

Still, Opal would have to face her sooner or later. Crystal Cove was too small to avoid someone forever. Better to get things out in the open now than letting days pass and awkwardly encountering her somewhere more public in town. Plus, Opal really did want Bonnie to know she had her support.

She knocked softly on the door in case Bonnie was still asleep so she wouldn't disturb her.

It seemed like forever before Opal heard sounds on the other side of the door.

A woman with a blond messy bun and dark shadows under her eyes answered. Jason's sister. The fact that she wasn't in pajamas was a good sign.

Opal offered a sympathetic smile. "Hello, Sally."

Sally studied her for a long moment, and awkwardness expanded between them. Sometime during her high school years when Sally had realized she'd never match her brother's excellence, Sally had stopped swimming and stopped socializing. Apparently not much had changed in her arena during Opal's time away.

"This isn't a good time, Opal."

Despite the chill coming off his sister, Opal's heart broke for her. "I know. That's why I'm here. I brought something for your mom."

A flicker of fury flashed in Sally's eyes. "This is all so unbelievable, you know. I don't know why she's so upset. It's not as if Jason brought her anything but heartache. She'll be better off without him."

An uncomfortable feeling rippled through Opal. Sally's response didn't make sense, and it certainly wasn't what Opal had expected when she'd knocked. "Excuse me?"

Sally released a dramatic exhale. "Let me see if she's up for a visitor."

She shut the door in Opal's face, and Opal blinked in surprise. Normally, folks in Crystal Cove were more polite and would at least leave the door open a bit, if not invite her in, but then again, these weren't normal times and Sally had always been odd.

Opal turned her gaze to the multi-pink columbines and delicate white peonies growing next to the house and watched as bees flitted from flower to flower. The insects were hard at work, engrossed in their own world and oblivious to hers. Most of the time, she lived the same way, but occasionally, she'd hear a voice in her head telling her to remember to live more fully in alignment with Mother Earth.

She always felt better when she listened.

The door opened, and Opal shifted her gaze and found Bonnie looking at her. Her eyes were red and swollen from crying, and her normally green aura had faded to a deep charcoal.

Opal reached a hand out to her, and Bonnie took it.

"Oh, Bonnie. I'm so sorry."

Fresh tears flooded the woman's eyes.

Opal didn't wait for an invitation but stepped forward and enveloped Bonnie in an embrace. She did her best to infuse love and light into the poor woman's bereaved heart.

She stepped back, closed the door behind her, and captured the lost look in Bonnie's eyes. "Let's sit down, okay? I brought you something, and I'd like to talk for a moment."

Bonnie lifted her brows. "Hank Halvorsen told me you found Jason. Is that true?"

Unexpected emotions tore at Opal's heart, and she nodded. "Let's sit."

She held tight to Bonnie's hand as they navigated their way to an olive-green couch covered with taupe and brown pillows. The woman had brought many of the colors of the earth inside, giving her home a relaxed, loving feeling.

Once they settled, Opal took both of Bonnie's hands in hers and looked into her eyes. Pain radiated in constant waves from her. "I'm not entirely sure what I'm supposed to say other than how very sorry I am about Jason. Yes, I did find him, and it tore me apart not being able to say anything to you when I saw you on the street."

Bonnie shook her head slowly. "I just...I don't understand why you didn't."

Opal squeezed Bonnie's hands and then released her. "Trust me. I wanted to tell you, but I also know there's a certain order to police procedures, and I needed to let that play out."

Bonnie's expression still seemed dazed. "That makes no sense to me."

Opal inhaled a slow breath and tried again. "What if I'd said something I shouldn't? What if I inadvertently released information that could jeopardize the investigation?"

Bonnie widened her eyes. "Investigation? Then it's not a suicide?"

It was Opal's turn to be surprised. "They think it might be a suicide?"

Her grandfather hadn't said a word.

"I don't know. Sally said some in town are speculating." Bonnie released a cry of anguish. "I just know my son is dead, and nothing will bring him back."

Opal had heard of witches long ago who'd supposedly been able to resurrect the dead, but that came with all kinds of black magic, something she was unwilling to touch. Otherwise, she'd be cursed forever because she'd bring back her mother, her grandmother, her childhood dog, and every other loved one who had or would pass.

No soul could withstand that kind of karma.

Opal scooted closer on the couch and wrapped an arm around Bonnie. She had to do something to help this woman, and she really believed her powers could provide her some relief. "I don't know anything more than you do now, Bonnie. I'm not privy to that information. But I can promise that if there's anything I can do to help you get answers, I will, okay?"

Bonnie nodded and wiped her eyes with the wad of tissues in her hand. "When Hank came to tell me the news, he asked if Jason had been having problems with anyone lately."

Opal yearned to ask what she'd told Hank, but her conscience kicked in to remind her that she was there to provide comfort. Not to use Bonnie for information.

Her heart fired back with a sincere reminder that anything she learned could be used to find out what happened to Jason and hopefully ease some of Bonnie's pain. Her heart argued that she only wanted to help, and therefore, it wasn't about knowing things for gossip's sake.

Bonnie needed an advocate.

Opal sat with that conviction for a few moments, giving her common sense a chance to respond. When no resistance came, she pressed forward, all in. "What did you say to Hank?"

Bonnie blinked her wet lashes several times, and Opal sensed the fight to control her emotions. "Well, obviously, Jason had his issues with Kandace. It's no secret their marriage didn't end well. Though I still think she cheated first."

Her interest piqued. This was the first Opal had heard of extra marital affairs, though she couldn't say she was surprised since they'd divorced. She didn't feel she could ask Bonnie for details, but she'd certainly ask Penelope what she knew.

Still, there was nothing wrong with skirting the edges of the subject. "I didn't mean to, but I overheard Vicky mention yesterday that Jason hadn't been paying his child support."

Bonnie heaved a weighted breath. "She's an awful person. Says she didn't want Jason and Kandace to divorce, but she did nothing to help them stay together either. She's always hated Jason for stealing her little girl."

Opal agreed with Bonnie's assessment of Vicky. She didn't need to use her senses to know that Kandace's mother wasn't a nice person. "I don't know Vicky very well, but she seemed extremely harsh with what she'd said about Jason."

"People don't understand. He's been through some rough times. After Tom Schofield opened a hotel hospitality business last year and undercut Jason's prices in order to steal his business, Jason really struggled to make ends meet. He didn't have the money to give to Kandace. I offered to have little Beau stay with me for a while so that Kandace didn't have to shoulder all the expenses, especially daycare, but she wouldn't hear of it. She rarely lets me see my Beau as it is."

Unfortunately, the more Bonnie talked, the more it seemed like Jason's death could be suicide. A desperate man with a grim future. It wasn't uncommon. "But Jason was trying to get back on his feet, right?"

Bonnie met her gaze with a heartfelt look. "He was. He truly was. I know my boy. He would never kill himself."

Opal yearned to know that for certain. Doing so would make investigating much easier. "I haven't seen Jason in years, but I find it hard to believe he would do such a thing, either."

Bonnie gave a righteous sniff. "And then there was that mess with Irina."

They obviously shared the same opinion about the woman. "Irina. She works for my grandfather."

Bonnie nodded. "From the first moment that I knew she and my son were dating, I told Jason she was trouble. Told him to stay away from her. Stupid man. He wouldn't listen, but anyone can see that she's all flash and no heart."

That had been Opal's experience, too, and she'd like nothing more than to pin a murder on Irina if she was guilty. But, Opal couldn't discount how distraught Irina had seemed to hear of Jason's passing. No one short of an academy award-winning actress could have pulled that off, in her opinion.

Opal wished she was better at reading someone's soul. "Trust me. I wouldn't mind a bit if Irina was involved, and she had to quit her job at the police station. Wouldn't cry if she went to jail. Unfortunately, she did seem devastated when she learned of his death."

Bonnie shook her head and met Opal's gaze with tear-filled eyes. "I need to know what happened, Opal. It's hard enough losing Jason, but so much worse without knowing why."

She curved her lips in sympathy. "You deserve answers, Bonnie. It won't bring him back, but you need to know."

Opal lifted the brown paper gift bag that had its handles tied with a sparkling sapphire blue ribbon and set it on Bonnie's lap. "I brought this for you."

A genuine, but small smile hovered on the woman's lips. "You didn't need to bring me anything. Your care and concern are enough."

Opal smiled. "Just open it."

Bonnie tugged on the ribbon, slid her hand inside the bag, and lifted the nature-infused candle to her nose. "It smells wonderful."

"Mulberry scented with rose hips and juniper in it. The rose will help lessen tension and stress, and juniper is for healing. Burn it whenever you need strength. It will bring peace to your heart."

Bonnie tucked the candle back into the bag. "Thank you for the kind gift."

Warmth from giving blossomed in Opal's heart. "You are so welcome. I learned to make them while I was away...at school. Someday, I'd like to open a gift shop to sell them."

The woman managed a kind smile. "If it's anything like you, your shop will be delightful."

Opal nodded and then stood. "I hate to leave so soon, but if I don't go now, I'll be late for my new job at the Rosewood Inn. Marla seems like an easygoing boss, but it won't look good for me to show up late on the first day."

Bonnie blinked wet lashes and stood. "You'll be good for Marla. She needs someone smart and organized."

Opal took both of her hands again and squeezed, excising more pain before she left. "I'd love it if you'd stop by the inn when you're feeling better and say hi. Also, please call if you need anything. I'm always available to help."

Bonnie placed a trembling hand on Opal's cheek and patted. "You're a good girl, Opal. Your mother would be proud of you."

Tender feelings opened inside Opal like they always did when someone mentioned her mother. It wasn't fair that they all were able to know her, but Opal couldn't. "You knew my mom."

Bonnie nodded sadly. "A wonderful woman. It's not okay, is it, that we lose the ones we love too early in life?"

Opal shook her head but couldn't speak. Instead, she hugged Bonnie, sending fierce love and gave her a small wave goodbye.

CHAPTER SIXTEEN

Pain rattled inside Opal as she drove the short distance to work. She wondered if there would come a day when she wouldn't miss her mother so much.

Instead of going directly inside the inn, she took a few extra moments to walk to the boardwalk and stand with her eyes closed while the strong ocean breeze blew through her soul.

Once Mother Nature had settled the ache inside her, Opal turned and strode toward the Rosewood Inn. Living a good life was the only gift she could give her mother, and she was determined to do that. She had a new job and new experiences to look forward to, and she would focus on those.

The stiff doorknob to the old inn groaned as she turned it, but the door opened without a sound. She lifted her chin, exhaled, and stepped inside. Mahogany wood, white lace curtains, and the scent of lemon polish greeted her.

Marla stood opposite the counter from Tom Schofield, writing something on a clipboard. Funny that Opal and Bonnie had just discussed him.

Opal studied him far more than she would have a day before. Tom was a year older than her, and he'd lost much of the hair he'd had when she'd left Crystal Cove years earlier. He'd always seemed like a decent guy.

Tom nodded to her in greeting. "Hi, Opal. Heard you were back."

Marla glanced up from the computer and smiled. "Hey, you. Good morning."

Her cheerfulness sent bright light into Opal's soul. "Good morning, to you both."

Marla slid the clipboard toward Tom. "Thanks again for the extra speedy delivery. I've been down a person, and it's hard to keep up with everything. Didn't realize we were almost out of shampoo. The good news is I've hired Opal to help, and she'll be amazing. Today is her first day."

Tom gave her a half-smile, picked up his clipboard, and called over his shoulder as he left. "Congratulations."

She faced her new boss. "I'm excited to start."

Marla motioned for Opal to join her behind the counter. "I don't have time to give you a formal training, so you'll just learn as we go. Sound okay?"

Opal nodded. "I'm up for the challenge."

"Good. I'll show you how to check guests in and out, and then I need to run to the store to purchase food for the upcoming week. It will likely be slow, since it's the middle of the week, so I also need you to inventory a shipment of supplies, guest soaps and other stuff, to make sure we received everything, and then put it away in the back office. Think you can handle that?"

Opal looked at the computer in front of her and then glanced into the backroom where three cardboard boxes rested on a table. "Sounds fairly simple."

Marla chuckled. "It is."

Her new boss slid the computer mouse across the surface of the counter and clicked on a screen. "We'll start with this couple who left early this morning. You'll just need to finalize their account."

Under Marla's tutelage, Opal followed her instructions and completed several client accounts. Then Marla picked up her cellphone, retrieved her purse from the backroom and headed out, leaving Opal in charge.

For a quick moment, Opal panicked, but then she reassured herself that she could handle the tasks. She could call Marla if she came across a difficult issue that couldn't wait.

Opal had just finished the computer work when a husband, wife, and their small child descended the stairs. The little daughter's tiny pink suitcase thumped each time it hit a wooden step. The father glanced at his wife, and she took the suitcase from the child.

The little girl with light blond curls protested loudly. "I can do it."

The mom looked to her daughter. "You're making too much noise, Amanda, and we don't want to damage the beautiful staircase."

Amanda let out a wail and ran to grab her father's legs as he descended the last step.

In an effort to avoid trampling the girl, he twisted awkwardly and hit hard against the wall. "Amanda," he scolded in a loud voice.

The little girl looked as though he'd broken her heart and continued to cry.

The man turned to his wife. "Take her outside. I'll settle up here."

Amanda protested loudly that she didn't want to leave the magic house, but her mother grabbed her wrist and tugged her outside anyway. The little pink suitcase made as much noise with the mother dragging it on its side.

Opal met the father's gaze and smiled. "Last name?"

The man scowled. "Pendleton."

Her nerves twisted as she typed in his name, and she hoped she didn't screw anything up that might make him angrier. "Pendleton. Yes. It looks like we just need to charge the last night to a credit card. Would you like me to use the one on file?"

He huffed his impatience. "Yes. Just hurry, please."

An unseen woman harrumphed. "What an unhappy, rude little family. Can you believe it, George?"

Opal glanced around but could see no one, and George, whoever he was, didn't respond.

Mr. Pendleton shot her an impatient look. "Is there a problem?"

Opal swallowed. "No, sir."

She quickly performed the necessary steps, printed his receipt, and handed it to him. "I hope you've enjoyed your stay and will come see us again."

He scoffed and swiped the paper from the desk. Without saying another word, he strode out, not shutting the door behind him.

Opal stared with her mouth half open and then made her way from behind the desk to close the door.

"Impertinent, ill-mannered oaf. His mother should have raised him better."

Opal swiveled around to discover who was speaking, but no one else was in the lobby. "Hello?" she called with a tentative voice.

When no one answered, she walked into the breakfast area in the adjoining room. But only two older gentlemen, one with a gray jacket and the other in a white shirt and tie sat at a back table sipping coffee. They looked up as she entered.

She gave them a warm smile. "Good morning."

They responded in kind.

Opal tilted her head to the side. She didn't want to ask, but she couldn't help herself. "Was there...a woman just in here with you?"

They glanced at each other and then back to her. "No," the one with the tie said. "Just us for the past twenty minutes or so."

She nodded politely. "I heard her speaking and wondered if she needed my help."

"I didn't hear anyone," he responded and then turned to the man in gray. "Did you?"

He shrugged at Opal. "Sorry, love. Didn't hear a thing."

She nodded, smiled again, and headed back to the front desk.

She hadn't imagined the voice. Couldn't have. Even though she had been thinking along the same lines when it came to that rude man.

The sound of a door slamming upstairs drew her gaze toward the ceiling. She stared for a long moment. Had she just encountered her first ghost?

She pondered for a minute and then chuckled.

"Couldn't be," she muttered under her breath.

****

The rest of Opal's morning passed without another incident from guests or possible resident ghosts. She mentioned her experience to Marla when she returned, but her boss only smiled and left Opal to draw her own conclusions, which furthered her curiosity.

When she walked out the door to take her lunch, she was still replaying the scene in her mind, searching for any detail she might have missed. She was so engrossed in her thoughts that she almost missed Lucas's police SUV parked on a side street. Not only that, but Lucas stood on the street corner diagonal to her, in deep conversation with a blond woman wearing high heels, tight jeans, and carrying a fashionable purse.

"*Kandace*," she hissed under her breath. She'd certainly changed from what Opal remembered.

Dang. She wished she was the one questioning Jason's ex-wife. If only she had some way to be invisible and sneak up on them.

Opal glanced across and down the street.

She couldn't directly approach them, but...if she was careful...she might be able to cross at the other end of the block and make her way back up, stopping just short of them seeing her and listen. They were far enough around the corner that if she stayed against the building it just might work.

Thoughts of lunch evaporated as Opal hurried to the end of the block. When traffic was clear, she strode across and then back toward the street corner. She paused near the store front closest to Lucas and Kandace and gazed inside at the selection of scarves and boots that decorated the boutique. For all anyone knew, she might be shopping.

She realized that if she tried, she could look through the window in front of her, through the corner of the store, and out another window on the other side and see them. She quickly stepped to the right where the window frame would hide her.

Lucas wouldn't be happy if he caught her. But she rationalized her spying because they were speaking in public and, therefore, had no right to expect privacy. Either way, she wasn't breaking any laws, and he couldn't ticket her.

He spoke first, sending a dangerous thrill through Opal. "I appreciate you talking to me here and what you've told me, but we will need you to come to the station so we can get an official record of your statement."

Kandace snorted. "I'm not going to do that, Lucas. I told you this is off the record. I had no way of knowing he hadn't taken my name off his insurance policy. I changed mine the day I filed for divorce."

"Hmm..." Lucas's voice rumbled in his chest. "I suppose he might have left you as beneficiary because you're the mother of his child."

"That would make sense to me. I am the one who's taking care of Beau, and Jason was so far behind in his child support payments. He probably felt guilty and wanted to give me the money for that."

Opal wished desperately that she could see their faces and use Kandace's expression to give her further clues on her honesty.

"I have to say," Lucas continued. "You don't seem to be particularly upset over the death of your son's father."

Kandace's angry vibrations were strong enough to reach Opal that time. "Tell me why I should be. He was a cheating, worthless jerk. I'm better off without him, and his son will be, too. I know everyone thinks he was the star of this town, but you all didn't know him like I did."

"Something you'd like to tell me about?" Lucas asked.

She hesitated for a long moment. "No. Nothing that will help now. The sooner his funeral comes and goes, the sooner we can put this all behind us."

Opal widened her eyes. Kandace *was* extremely cold when it came to her ex-husband. The urge to see Kandace's face encouraged Opal to take a quick peek. She tilted her head to the side, and found Lucas staring intently at Kandace. Unfortunately, with their current positions, she could only see Kandace's shoulder-length, white-blond hair and the profile of her chin and nose.

"Has Bonnie scheduled the funeral date yet? The chief and I would like to attend," Lucas said.

Kandace sighed. "She hasn't let me know yet."

Lucas shifted, and his gaze brushed past Opal and then returned with lightning speed. She blinked and then focused on a fantastic pair of red suede boots. Then, without glancing his direction again, she turned and strode away from them.

She knew he'd seen her, but he couldn't know that she'd overheard or how long she'd been there. She wasn't about to stick around and have him question her.

Opal made it half a block before she heard him call her name. She groaned but didn't stop.

A rush of footsteps and a firm hand on her shoulder told her the game was over. She turned to face her consequences.

CHAPTER SEVENTEEN

Opal looked into Lucas's frustrated eyes and prepared for the worst.

"Didn't you hear me?" he demanded.

She placed the most innocent look she could on her face and blinked. "Oh, sorry. I guess I wasn't paying attention."

He narrowed his gaze. "You're a terrible liar."

She scoffed in offense. "Excuse me?"

A knowing smile twisted his lips, and he shook his head. "That's not going to work with me. I know you were eavesdropping on my conversation with Kandace. Don't try to deny it."

Opal searched for a plausible reason to explain her presence but came up with nothing. "Fine. Maybe I did overhear something, but you both were talking in plain daylight on a public street. It's not my fault."

He chuckled and shook his head again. "Not your fault? Huh. Okay. I guess I can't argue with that. But it's still considered rude in Crystal Cove to sneak up on someone and listen in."

She straightened her spine. "I didn't sneak."

"Oh, yes. You did. I saw you only moments before heading down the opposite side of the street. A minute later, you were near me."

His look dared her to challenge his claim.

"I'd forgotten what I was shopping for," she offered weakly.

A disappointed look darkened his irises. "The worst thing you can do, Opal, is lie to me."

His barb hit home. She prided herself on being a good, honest person.

She folded her arms and sighed in defeat. "Fine. I was eavesdropping. But it's only because you won't tell me anything."

A hint of a smile appeared on his lips, letting her know he approved of her admission of guilt. "That's because it's an official police investigation. I believe we've discussed this."

She stared at him, hating the corner he'd backed her into. "I'm not asking for confidential information."

He lifted a questioning brow. "You're not?"

"No...I'm asking for speculation. That's all. Just your opinion. Nothing that could be confidential."

He studied her for a long moment, and she assumed he was looking for a loophole in her request that might hang him later. "I don't know, Opal. Still seems like I'm crossing a line."

She bit her bottom lip and switched tactics. "I have your jacket in my car and need to return it to you."

A relieved expression brightened his face. He thought she was letting him off the hook. "Oh, okay."

"On one condition."

He dropped his shoulders. "I can't talk about the investigation, Opal."

She sent him a flirty smile. "I want to know if you know about Kandace's affair."

The air tightened around them. "Affair?"

So, he didn't know.

"Bonnie told me, and I wondered if you knew who she'd been seeing, and if they've been together after the divorce."

He lifted a shoulder and let it drop. "Jason had publicly accused her of it, but that was after he'd been caught with Irina, so no one believed him."

Interesting. "Who did people say she'd been with?"

He hesitated.

She shot him a sarcastic look. "I'm not asking anything confidential. Ninety-five percent of the people in town could likely answer that question."

He shifted his weight, and she knew she'd won that round.

"Tom Schofield."

She dropped her mouth open. "What? I just saw Tom this morning."

She tried to wrap her brain around the idea of the two of them as a couple. Scrawny, balding guy and hot blonde? "I can't exactly picture them together."

"Neither could anyone else, which is why the rumor died quickly."

So much for intriguing information. Her brain had been prepared to run with the idea, but it was like a kite on a windless day going nowhere.

Another thought popped into her head, and she frowned. "Bonnie also mentioned Tom was undercutting Jason's prices, and that it had hurt Jason's business significantly."

Lucas tipped his head in agreement. "That's what I understand."

She couldn't quite let go of the idea. "So, there was a rivalry of sorts?"

"Of sorts."

Two black marks against Tom. Now, that was something she could sink her teeth into.

She playfully linked her arm with Lucas's and steered him in the direction of her car. "Let's talk while we walk. My car is parked around the corner from the Rosewood Inn."

He chuckled. "Does that mean I'm getting my jacket back?"

She grinned. "Of course. Besides, it's already caused me enough trouble."

"Your grandfather?"

"How did you—" she began but stopped. "Never mind. You know this because he talked to you."

He shrugged. "I can handle it. The guys are giving me grief, but it's worth it to know you weren't cold."

His declaration stunned her, and she glanced up at him. He smiled, and her heart did a weird flutter thing that she hadn't expected. "Umm...thank you, I guess?"

She wasn't sure how to respond. The guys were teasing him, but he didn't care? Should she care?

She was grateful to reach her car and gently disengage her arm from his. Suddenly, things seemed more serious and not so playful.

She unlocked the Mustang and reached inside for his jacket. When she straightened, she glanced down the street and found her ex-boyfriend, still with the same shaggy blond hair and irritatingly attractive swagger, walking toward them with a genuine smile on his face. The last time she'd seen Ryan Gallagher, she'd left a handprint on his right cheek.

Instead of greeting her first, Ryan extended his hand to Lucas. "Good to see you, bro."

She blinked. *Bro?*

She sensed that Lucas had dropped his guard, and he gave Ryan's hand a friendly shake. "What's up, dude?"

Ryan focused wary eyes on Opal. "Heard this lady was back in town. Wanted to say hi."

The biggest reason she hadn't made her way back to Crystal Cove in six years stood in front of her. Before Ryan had broken her heart, Opal had expected to come home every few months to see her grandpa and the man who she'd thought was the love of her life. She'd also only planned to be gone for two years.

But then she'd caught Ryan drunker than a cursed skunk at a beach party, making out with Tracie Frost. He'd been so drunk that she'd stood in front of them watching for a full ten seconds before he'd noticed. When he'd finally managed to get to his feet, her parting gift had been a slap on the cheek and harsh words that he should never try to contact her again.

Opal had gotten over him after two months, and her friends had assured her that he'd been nothing but a flash in the cauldron. Without Ryan waiting for her to come home and with her grandpa encouraging her to stay in Sedona, she'd had no reason to rush back to Crystal Cove.

The absence of anger in her heart told her they'd been right. She managed a smile without much trouble. "Hello, Ryan."

Lucas glanced between them with his eyebrows drawn down. "You know each other?"

Ryan started to answer, but Opal cut him off with a quick laugh. "Crystal Cove *is* a small town. It would be more surprising if we didn't."

The last thing she wanted was for Ryan to remind everyone what had transpired between them. The past was better left in the past, and if the man knew what was good for him, he'd take the cue and let dead things rest in peace.

"Guess you're right," Lucas responded, seeming satisfied.

Ryan snorted. "Oh, come on, Opal. I know it's been a while, but you remember all the good times we had. We shared more than a town."

Her cheeks heated, and she shot laser-focused daggers in his direction. "Might think twice before you bring up events that don't portray you in the best light."

Lucas widened his eyes in interest, but she didn't intend on divulging more. Nor did she plan on spending more time in Ryan's company. She thrust Lucas's jacket into his arms and shut her car door.

She sensed Ryan's good cheer fizzle, and a wicked thought crossed her mind. Some might call her idea returning fire. She stood on tiptoe and kissed Lucas's cheek. "Thank you for the loan last night. I need to get back to work before I'm late."

Her lips burned from their contact, leaving her unsettled.

She turned from both men and hurried down the sidewalk as fast as she could without running. She didn't spare either of them a glance as she turned the corner and made a beeline for the inn. Truth be told, she had really wanted to see Ryan's expression. If he somehow thought he had a chance with her, he was dead wrong.

But she didn't dare look back, afraid of what she might find in Lucas's eyes. She couldn't deny an odd, intense connection between them, but the fact was, if he hadn't appreciated her kiss, she didn't want to know.

Worse, if he had, she didn't want to know the effects of the ripple in the universe she'd just created. If she'd only waited a second or two before acting, she would have foreseen the folly of her actions.

Now, it was too late to take back her kiss.

CHAPTER EIGHTEEN

Every second of the afternoon crawled by at a starfish's pace until Opal's shift at the Rosewood Inn was finally over. The skies had darkened while she'd been inside, and a light sprinkle of rain greeted her as she emerged. But the moisture wasn't enough to keep her from walking the two blocks to Sammy's Tsunami Sweet Shop rather than drive.

The delicious smell of fresh-made ice cream cones welcomed her inside. She ordered two scoops each for Penelope and her of cherry chocolate chip ice cream. She'd just finished paying when Penelope entered the shop. Her friend's cheeks were pink from walking briskly from the clothing shop where she worked, and Opal imagined hers were the same.

Penelope pushed the periwinkle hood from her head and ran a hand over her short, dark hair. She glanced at the cones in Opal's hands and laughed. "Two scoops?"

Opal settled her features into a solemn expression. "Serious problems call for serious measures."

Penelope's smile grew bigger. "Apparently, this is going to be a doozy. I can't wait to hear what you've done now."

They took their cones to a corner bistro table and sat on the red-cushioned ice cream parlor chairs.

Opal licked the melting edges from her ice cream and then focused on Penelope. "I kissed Lucas Keller."

Penelope choked on a swallow. *"You did what?"*

The severity of what she really had done slammed Opal harder than ice cream would likely cure. "Not a romantic kiss. Just a kiss on the cheek."

Penelope lifted her brows. "But you put your lips on him. You don't even know him that well."

Opal snorted in despair. "If by knowing him well, you mean approximately forty-eight hours, then yes, you are correct."

Her friend licked her cone and then focused a confused gaze on Opal. "What were the cosmic events that led to this outcome?"

"Ryan." She spat the word. "Apparently, Lucas and he are friends."

Opal spilled the complete story, ending with the kiss and a knot in her stomach.

A guilty look crossed Penelope's face. "Yeah, they've been friends for a while."

She couldn't believe it. "Why didn't you say something?"

Penelope held up a hand in protest. "I didn't say anything because a few days ago, you didn't even know who Lucas was, and I wasn't about to bring up Ryan's name. Besides, how the heck was I supposed to know you'd end up in a three-way conversation with the two of them. Or worse, that you'd think it was a good idea to kiss Lucas to make Ryan jealous."

"I thought you were psychic," Opal responded in frustration.

Penelope widened her eyes in offense. "Say you're sorry."

Opal dropped her shoulders. "I am sorry. That was mean and uncalled for."

Opal knew as well as Penelope that magical gifts were rarely available on-demand. At least for people at their skill levels. "I just don't understand what's happening here. I shouldn't be having conversations with either of them. One broke my heart, and the other gave me a speeding ticket. These are not men I want in my life."

The two attacked their ice cream for several moments in silence before a bright smile hit Penelope's lips. "I know. You need to find a way to make Ryan forget he ever knew you."

A glimmer of hope lit inside Opal. She leaned closer to Penelope and spoke in a low voice. "You mean like a spell? A forgetful spell?"

Penelope nodded. "Why not? You're a witch. I would think there's such a spell."

Opal sighed. "Yeah, but unfortunately, I didn't learn that one. Some of the witches offered to use it on me when I first arrived in Sedona and I couldn't function beyond my heartbreak, but I was too scared to mess with things back then."

"Still, that sounds perfect. Can you call one of them and ask how to do it?"

Opal's mood improved immensely. "Yes. That should be easy, actually. I can make Ryan forget he knew me, and then it will be like none of that ugliness ever happened."

Penelope grinned. "This is why we will always be friends. You need me too much."

Opal chuckled. "You aren't kidding. I don't know what I'd do without you, which brings me to the other reason I wanted to talk to you."

Penelope nodded wisely. "I thought there might be something else. I knew you'd call this afternoon, but for whatever odd reason, I thought it would be about Tom Schofield."

Opal straightened in her seat and honed her senses, scanning Penelope's aura for anything magical. And there it was, small sparks igniting just along the fringes. "You had a vision about us?"

She shrugged. "I think so. I mean I imagined us meeting, but I didn't foresee two scoops of ice cream or anything about Ryan."

A crazy idea formed in Opal's thoughts, and excitement skittered through her veins. "What did we talk about in your vision?"

Her expression fell. "I don't know. I didn't get further than a glimpse of us together and the impression it was about Tom."

Opal exhaled a deep breath, hoping she could convince Penelope to help her. "Okay, this is totally weird, but our conversation just gave me another idea. Hear me out."

Opal waited for Penelope's approval before she continued. "Some have hinted Jason might have killed himself, but it's looking more and more like the police don't believe that theory. This is totally confidential, so don't say anything to anyone, but Tom Schofield is a person of interest in Jason's case. He and Kandace have been rumored to have had an affair while she was still married."

Penelope blinked and leaned forward. "Oh...now that *is* interesting. I do remember something about them a while back."

Her friend paused for a moment. "I could maybe see Tom being guilty. I mean, he does give off a shifty vibe."

Opal snickered. "Shifty vibe? Really?"

That hadn't been her experience with him at the inn. "Anyway," Opal continued. "I had this thought just a second ago. There is a truth-telling spell that I learned. You have to make a person drink something, which might prove difficult in Tom's case, but what do you think? Should we give it a try and see what he tells us?"

Penelope blinked her bright blue eyes several times. "Are you kidding? I'd love to help you try a spell. That would be amazing."

Opal laughed. "You're crazier than I thought."

"Uh...you're the one suggesting we drug someone."

She gasped. "We're not drugging him."

Penelope shrugged. "What's the difference? We're giving him something he doesn't know about that will cause a reaction that he's not consenting to."

Opal frowned. Knowing which lines to cross and not cross and the karma that could accompany them wasn't always so easy to navigate. "It's only a simple, small spell, and it's for a good reason. If he's a murderer, he deserves it. If not, then we'll know it wasn't him."

Penelope lifted both hands. "You don't have to justify anything to me. I'm all in."

She supposed she'd have to accept the consequences if there were any. "Okay. Let me figure out the logistics, and I'll let you know when and how."

"Sweet."

Opal nodded and drifted into her thoughts. The fact that she was doing it for a good cause and selfless reasons should protect her from negative karma. She hoped.

But what if it didn't?

CHAPTER NINETEEN

Next morning, the sun was out, and the weatherman had forecasted a cloudless day, a rarity on the Oregon Coast. Luckily, Opal had planned to volunteer at the police station for a few hours that morning, and she didn't have to be at the Rosewood until late afternoon. She arrived at the police station bright and early, with a box of Malcolm's fresh donuts in hand.

Irina greeted her with an unfriendly smile that left apprehension in Opal's heart. She wanted to have sympathy for the woman. She really did. But Irina carried her nastiness like a badge of honor. It wouldn't surprise Opal if she had something to do with Jason's death.

Still, she'd try for some semblance of kindness for peace's sake. "Good morning."

Opal lifted the box she carried. "I brought donuts if you'd like one."

Irina snorted. "I don't eat junk food."

She hardly considered donuts to be junk food. The term, junk, was reserved for unwanted things. Donuts were far from that.

Opal shrugged at Irina, acting as if she could care less. Plenty of the guys would want one, and she set the box of goodies on a counter near the coffee pot where they would notice them. Coffee steamed as she filled her cup, and then she slipped a chocolate-covered donut onto a napkin. She considered closing the lid but decided to torture Irina with scents of fresh-baked goodness.

Irina turned back to her computer. A second later, she glanced at Opal again. "Are you going to be here *all* day?"

Annoyance dripped from her words and grated against Opal's nerves. She wanted to say yes just to annoy her but couldn't. "I told my grandpa I'd help organize his office for a few hours this morning."

"So, you won't be in my hair?"

Opal sent her an overly-sweet smile. "No. I won't have to look at you, and you won't have to look at me."

She didn't wait for a response before heading into the chief's office. He was already out on a call, so that was a bonus, too. She hated being at odds with the man, especially since they'd spent so much time apart, but today was not the day she wanted to work to fix it. She had enough to think about already.

Opal took several moments to try to decipher the system he had in place and then gave up. The man obviously stored things willy-nilly, with no rhyme or reason at all. She figured she might as well start with his desk drawers, and she began to pull everything out and set it on his desk.

When she came across a photo of her as a child holding a sea star and wearing the biggest, toothy smile, an ache rippled through her. She missed the man who'd taken such good care of her as a child, and she needed to find a way to connect their hearts once again.

"Excuse me."

Opal startled and glanced up. If her pulse hadn't already been galloping from fright, the sight of the handsome, yet annoying officer would have jolted her anyway.

She hadn't come to grips with how she'd act when she saw Lucas again after her rogue kiss, so her body decided heated cheeks was the answer. "Lucas. Hi."

One for the books as far as clever statements went. Not.

"Do you have a second?" he asked.

She swallowed and nodded. If only she could sense something about him, she might have an idea of where this conversation would lead.

He closed the office door and sent her currently useless senses on high-alert. She remained sitting, and he walked to the corner of the desk so that she had to look up to see him.

He met her gaze with a serious look. "I wanted to talk to you about what happened yesterday."

She slid the chair back and stood. "I'm sorry. I shouldn't have kissed you. I barely know you, and I don't make it a habit of kissing strange men."

He narrowed his gaze ever so slightly. "I wouldn't exactly call us strangers."

His words scattered her thoughts, confusing her. Was he defending her actions? "Either way, I don't usually kiss men I barely know."

He shrugged. "Don't worry about it. I figured it was a thank you kiss. Nothing to get worked up over."

Her hackles rose. "I'm not worked up over it. I just—"

She exhaled a slow breath and tried again. "What exactly did you want to talk to me about?"

"Ryan."

She rolled her eyes in disgust. "I have nothing to say about that man."

"He said you'd dated. For quite a while."

She folded her arms. "I don't see how that's any of your business, nor why we are discussing him."

Lucas placed a warm hand on her shoulder, and she froze. Electricity coursed through her in rivulets. "He told me you are a witch."

Icy wariness splashed through her like a wintry waterfall. She took a step back, and he dropped his hand.

Had he closed the door to keep her from attempting an escape? "Are you a hunter like my grandfather?" she asked quietly.

He stared at her for a long moment. "Do you mean do I hunt witches and other paranormals?"

She nodded.

He glanced at the door as though to make sure it was firmly closed. "No, Opal. I don't. But that's why I wanted to talk to you. I'm worried about you. I know that we have a few hunters who pass through this way from time to time. Some who come looking specifically for your grandfather, wanting his advice or to hear his stories."

She nodded again. "I know. We used to have them show up at the house, and my grandfather would make me hide."

He drew his brows down, creasing his forehead. "That was a little dangerous, wasn't it?"

She shrugged. "My grandpa always kept me safe."

He exhaled a deep sigh. "I guess I need to remember he wasn't always like he is now."

It was her turn to frown. "What's that supposed to mean?"

Lucas held up a hand as a sign of peace. "Nothing to get riled up about. Just that he's slowing down a little. It will happen to all of us."

Him telling her not to get upset had the opposite effect. "I'm not *riled* up."

He lifted a challenging brow, deepening her annoyance.

She breathed to slow her pulse. "Well, I wasn't until you accused me of it. Maybe you should get to the point of your visit before you make me really angry."

A grin tilted his lips. "And what? You'll hex me?"

It wasn't a bad idea. "Now, you're mocking me."

"Sorry. I do that without realizing it, especially to people I like. I wanted to tell you to talk to Ryan about opening his mouth. I already did, but you should, too. I'm not sure why you told him about your heritage in the first place. He made it sound like he wasn't the most trustworthy guy."

She dropped her jaw. First, Lucas told her he liked her and then questioned her ability to know who to trust. Granted, hindsight proved him right, but she hadn't been reckless with her personal information back in the day. She'd loved Ryan.

Or at least thought she had. "Wow. Exactly how many insults are you prepared to fire at me?"

He seemed surprised. "I wasn't. Ryan's the one with the problem."

"Except you questioned my sanity in telling him. Not to mention, what I do in my personal life is my business. Not yours."

Her words kept him quiet for several moments, and she figured he was probably replaying what he'd said to make her angry. "You're right. I apologize for overstepping."

Her anger fizzled without her approval, and she dropped into her grandpa's chair. "Thanks for letting me know. I'll talk to him."

A lift of his chin was the only acknowledgement he gave her. He walked to the door, glanced at her once more and then left.

And now, she felt like an idiot.

She worked to push that out of her mind. She had bigger things to worry about. Lucas was right. She needed to talk to Ryan immediately, before things spiraled further out of control.

She'd do it today, in fact. No time like the present.

Opal flicked a quick glance to her bag sitting on the desk, and her special, leather-bound spell book that her mentor, Tara, had brought back from Scotland for her. Opal had always been jealous of the old, family tomes with generations of spells that others had at their disposal. She wished she had her mother's or grandmother's, but her grandfather had told her he'd burned them shortly after their deaths.

In light of that, she accepted she'd be starting a new line, a new book of spells that could be passed down to her children someday.

She hastily put the contents of her grandfather's desk back together. They weren't as organized as she would have liked if she'd had more time. But she suddenly had a more important matter to attend to now.

While the office was still quiet, she slipped her spell book from her bag and opened to the freshly-inked page and the spell she'd written from the previous night when she'd called Tara.

The Forgetful Spell would be harder than many she'd practiced since it invoked a greater power to complete. Luckily, she wasn't trying to make Ryan forget everything he knew. Only things related to her.

Honestly, it would be best for everyone, so Karma shouldn't hold it against her.

CHAPTER TWENTY

Opal strode across the firm sand, toward the sea cave. Erasing a man's memory wasn't how she'd planned to spend the sunny day, but at least she was out in the elements and could absorb the fantastic energy. Also, the power of the sun should help to strengthen her spell and ensure that it worked.

The cool, damp interior of the cave calmed her fears. She scattered small pieces of wood she'd gathered in preparation for her spell and then sat on one of the boulders protruding from the sand. This was the spot, when she'd been younger, where she'd tried her first unsuccessful spells. She'd found a resurrection spell online and had tried to bring her mother back to life.

The spell had done nothing except make her vomit and lose massive strands of hair. At the time, she'd been so disappointed, but now she could see it was a blessing that the spell hadn't worked.

Opal sensed Ryan before he entered the cave, and she was glad that he'd accepted her invitation. She only wished she could read Lucas as well. Maybe that would come once she knew him better.

She glanced up as Ryan walked in. A slight shiver skittered through her, a bare fraction of emotion from the olden days, and her traitorous heart beat faster. Ninety-nine percent of the time, the sight of him had meant wonderful moments. But she needed to remember the other one percent that had shattered her naïve heart.

He lifted a hand. "Hey, Opal."

She steadied her nerves. "Hi, Ryan."

He walked closer and perched on one of the large rocks near her. "I was surprised you called. Even more surprised you wanted to come back to one of our old haunts. The way you acted yesterday, I was sure you'd never want to see me again."

He wasn't wrong there. "Crystal Cove is too small to avoid you forever. I thought it might be better to make peace."

He curved his lips into the boyish smile she'd always loved. "Peace is a beginning."

Not the kind of beginning he was expecting though.

She returned his smile. "You broke my heart, you know."

All traces of happiness disappeared from his face, and he gave a solemn nod. "I know. I broke mine, too. It was the biggest mistake of my life."

The words she'd longed to hear for months after she'd left Crystal Cove pierced her heart. "I want to know why. I thought we loved each other. Thought we were planning a life together."

He dropped his gaze and shook his head. "I don't know, Opal. I guess I freaked out because you were leaving. I had all these crazy ideas in my head of how you'd change, that you'd become so powerful and wouldn't want a simple guy like me."

She considered his words for a moment and wondered if he might have been right. She certainly wasn't the same girl as she'd been before.

He tilted his head up and caught her gaze. "I think I was wrong, though. You seem like the same beautiful girl I've always known. Maybe even more beautiful."

A blush warmed her cheeks, and she cursed it. "Flattery isn't going to get you anywhere."

He lifted his brows, and his eyes sparkled. "No?" he asked in a teasing voice.

Something powerful inside her came to life and responded. "No."

Their time had passed. They'd taught each other whatever life had intended, and they needed to look toward the future. She would ensure that would happen.

She smiled coyly. "Did you know I've been coming to this place since I was a child?"

He shook his head. "I thought it was our special spot."

"It was. It's also the place I tried my first spell."

A nervous look came into his eyes. "Did you learn a lot of spells while you were away?"

She shrugged. "A few. Most of my training included respecting Mother Earth, the connections between everything on our planet, and how someone can draw energy from that."

He relaxed a little then. "That doesn't seem too crazy."

She smiled. "Nope. In fact, all of it seemed very peaceful and positive to me."

She focused a sharp gaze on him until she was certain she had his full attention. "Would you like to see me do a spell?"

His nervousness returned. "Depends. Is it a good one or bad?"

She chuckled. "Don't worry. I never mess with dark magic, and I never do a spell that's not for the greater good of everyone."

Seriously, though. Erasing his memories would be the best for them both.

He stretched his legs out in front of him, and sand fell from the bottoms of his shoes. "Okay. Show me what you've got."

Her nerves balled into a tangled mass, and she tried to reassure herself that she could manage things. She wasn't a novice. Hadn't been for many years.

She gathered the twigs she'd conveniently placed around the cave and laid them in a pile.

"Wet sticks don't burn, Opal."

She smiled sweetly. First off, they weren't wet, but she wouldn't tell him that. "Doesn't matter when magic is involved," she lied.

She reached into her pocket and removed four crystals. She placed an aquamarine for water, a carnelian for fire, an agate for earth, and lastly, a moonstone for air at the north, south, west and east points of her small area. "These enhance my magic."

Ryan continued to watch with interest but didn't speak.

Opal took a deep breath and silently prayed she'd do the spell correctly. "Mother Earth, please spare us pain. Remove all memory of me from his brain."

He straightened on the rock. "Wait. What?"

"Fill the space with a golden void."

He jumped to his feet and reached for her. "No, Opal."

"Only times with me will be destroyed. This I ask, so mote it be."

The ground shook beneath her feet, and the sand liquified around them.

He reached for her, caught her arm, and pulled her into his embrace. His eyes filled with pain. "Why?"

She wasn't sure exactly how long it would be before the spell took effect, and she didn't dare pull away. "It was never meant to be, Ryan. We both know that."

He shook his head in denial and then captured her lips with his. The kiss sparked and then died. A second later, he crumpled to her feet, out cold.

"Oh, crap," she whispered.

She dropped next to him and patted his face repeatedly. "Ryan? Ryan. Wake up."

Tara hadn't mentioned this part of the spell. What if she couldn't get him to respond? She didn't have long until the tide would come in and fill the cave.

Good Gaia. She could have unknowingly just killed the man.

The thought infused her with stark fear.

"Ryan?" she yelled this time. "Wake up."

He took a deep breath and blinked his eyes.

Relief flooded her, and she fell to her bottom on the sand next to him. "I'm so glad you're okay."

He glanced around, confused. "Where am I?"

She swallowed. "The old sea cave on the south end of the beach."

He raised himself to his elbows and looked around. "I...don't remember coming in here."

That was a good sign.

He sat up and glanced at his clothes. "I wasn't surfing, so I have no idea why I'd be at the beach. I must have passed out or something."

"Oh? You surf?" she asked as though she didn't know.

He nodded and then placed hands on both sides of his head. "Man, that hurts."

She silently asked for his forgiveness. "We'd better get you out of here before the tide comes in. Do you think you can stand?"

With her help, he got to his feet.

"Feel steady enough?" she asked.

He wrapped an arm about her shoulders for support and nodded. "Yeah."

She slipped her arm around his waist and directed him toward the cave entrance. All she had to do was get him out of harm's way, and then she could go for help if she needed to.

They were almost to the soft sand before he spoke again. "What's your name?"

The question took her by surprise. Then again, if he was asking, her spell must have worked. "I'm Opal."

Guilt nipped her. "What's yours?"

"Ryan," he said and rubbed his free hand across his head, encouraging the breeze to toss his blond hair. "I think I must have hit my head really hard."

She grimaced. "I'm sure you'll feel better in no time."

"Yeah. Maybe. It's just so weird."

He dropped his gaze to her, and she tried hard not to look away. "You saved my life, you know?"

"No," she answered immediately.

"Yeah, if you hadn't come along, I might not have woken up and could have drowned."

She didn't know what to say. If she argued too much, she might seem suspicious. "I'm glad I could help."

As they neared the boardwalk, she caught sight of a lone figure standing next to the cement wall separating beach from land. At first, she thought it was a man staring out to sea, but she realized it was Lucas, and he wasn't looking at the ocean.

He was watching them.

From Lucas's point of view, she and Ryan probably looked like a couple enjoying a romantic stroll. Which was so far from the truth that it was ridiculous.

Before they were close enough for her to call out to him to help with Ryan, Lucas turned and strode away.

Opal looked toward the heavens to ask for mercy, and instead found dark clouds building over the mountain to the east. A low buzz in the air warned her to be careful of what was to come.

She wanted to ask Mother Earth for more specific instructions but couldn't with Ryan walking beside her.

They made their way past the cement wall to the boardwalk, and Opal dug in her heels so that they'd stop walking. She searched Ryan's features, looking for signs of distress. "Doing okay?"

He nodded and smiled as though relieved. "Much better. Headache's mostly gone. Don't really feel dizzy much anymore, either."

Thank the earth and stars. "I'm *so* happy to hear that."

He grinned. "You're my guardian angel. You saved me and made me feel better."

She shook her head vehemently. "Oh, no. Don't say that. I was just lucky to be in the right place at the right time to help you. Could have been anyone."

He touched the tip of her nose, and she blinked. "But it wasn't. It was you. Are you visiting Crystal Cove?"

A flutter of panic rolled through her. She hadn't anticipated him wanting to get to know her all over again. "I actually just came home from being away at school. I live with my grandpa, Police Chief Winston."

He frowned. "I know the chief really well. How come I don't know you?"

She sent him a mock, embarrassed smile. "Oh, you know. I was one of those awkward girls in high school that no one noticed."

He gave her a once-over before meeting her eyes again. "You're anything but awkward now."

She faked a chuckle. "Thanks. Uh...now that you're okay, I should be on my way."

She couldn't get out of there soon enough.

He snatched her hand. "Wait. I want to take you for ice cream to thank you."

The last thing she needed was more ice cream and the opportunity to come up with harebrained ideas. "Sorry. I don't have time right now. I need to be at work soon."

Which was the truth.

She tugged her hand from his, and he reluctantly let go. "Okay, my angel. Next time for sure."

She gave him a wide smile without agreeing and turned from him. One step and then two steps, and then she was practically running. Ryan might notice and take offense, but she really didn't care. She'd banished him from her life and intended to keep things that way.

CHAPTER TWENTY-ONE

Two days later, Opal spotted Penelope's car parked near the corner of Main and Second Street, and she pulled in next to her. She retrieved the drink holder that carried three coffees and exited her car. A few seconds later, she slid onto Penelope's passenger seat.

Opal sent her friend a worried look. "I'm totally rethinking the idea of using the truth-telling spell on Tom. After the disaster with Ryan, I'm a little leery of trying spells on anyone else. Helping flowers to grow or creating balms like my friend taught me is one thing. Even protective spells would be fine but messing with people's heads might be out of my league for now."

Penelope rolled her eyes and twisted a coffee from the cardboard holder. "I don't know what you're talking about. To me, it sounds like your spell worked perfectly. Ryan has no memories of your past, so you can forget it, too."

She tried to buy into Penelope's version of what had happened, but something in her gut told her things were not that simple.

Opal exhaled a breath full of worry. "I did mention to Marla that it might be nice to upgrade the type of soaps and shampoos she offers. I read that people love to feel spoiled on vacation and adding a few small touches can do that without costing tons. Then she could charge more for the rooms, too."

Penelope sipped her coffee. "Did she agree?"

Opal gave a small shrug. "She said I could look into it and give her a price breakdown."

"Then we're all set to visit Tom, right?"

Apprehension filled Opal. "I guess so."

Penelope gestured toward the leather-bound book poking out of Opal's bag. "When do we perform the spell? Uh, I mean, when do you?"

Opal eyed her friend with a sideways look. "Are you sure you aren't agreeing to this just because you want to watch me work magic? Because if that's all it is, I can come up with a spell you'd enjoy more."

Penelope widened her eyes into innocent ovals. "No. This is important work, remember? We both said we thought our skills would come in handy for the police department. You have something to prove to your grandfather, and this is the perfect way to start."

She snorted. "I highly doubt he'd let me cast a spell on every possible suspect that he comes across."

Penelope shrugged. "I would if I was him. He'd have a one-hundred percent catch rate, and if he'd let me help him, we might be able to stop crimes from happening in the first place. Really, he wouldn't need any of his officers anymore if he had us. We'd be a superhero duo."

Opal laughed for the first time in days. "You really are off your rocker."

Penelope beamed a bright smile. "The best people are."

Opal resigned herself to giving Tom a witch version of a polygraph. If it yielded great results, she might dare to approach her grandfather again. "Okay, just so we're on the same page. We stopped for coffee and a new barista poured an extra and then just gave it to us, right? We needed to stop by Tom's shop, so we figured we'd give it to him."

"Yes." Penelope nodded firmly. "That's exactly right."

Opal groaned in resistance and pulled a small clear bottle from her purse. "I hope he likes milk and a touch of vinegar in his coffee."

"You put lots of sugar and cream in, too, right? To help mask the taste?" Penelope asked.

Opal couldn't believe she was doing an intermediate spell for the second time in two weeks. "His coffee is all doctored up, so hopefully he won't taste it at all."

She handed the small bottle to Penelope, lifted the lid off Tom's coffee, and reluctantly pulled out her spell book. She opened it to the correct page and took back the small bottle. "Mother Earth, please watch over me as I attempt this spell."

"Amen," Penelope added.

Opal glanced at her with raised brows.

"What?" Penelope responded in a defensive tone. "I'm just trying to help."

Opal closed her eyes and cleared her mind. She repeated the words she'd memorized, surprised that she didn't experience the same fears she had with Ryan's spell.

When she was finished, she opened her eyes and poured the contents into the extra-large, loaded coffee and then turned her gaze to Penelope. "Drive. The potency of this spell doesn't last long. If we were to use a truth-telling candle instead, it would cost me a day of my life."

Penelope shook her head. "This spell will be just fine."

Penelope pulled into the parking lot of Tom's Toiletries and Hotel Supply. She gripped Opal's forearm before she could open the car door. "I'm so excited. I just know this is going to work."

Opal gave her a wary glance. "Did you have a vision?"

Penelope shook her head. "No, but I feel it in my bones."

"I wish my bones were as certain as yours."

Together they exited the car, bringing their coffees as well as Tom's. A bell tinkled as they opened the door to the house-turned-business office. In the front of the building was a small counter and an old metal desk sitting not far behind it. Opal could only describe the smell of the place as clean.

Despite the bell on the door, no one came to the front of the old house.

Opal's nerves kicked into high gear. "Maybe he's not here."

Penelope frowned her disappointment. "Of course, he's here. His car is parked outside, and the door was unlocked," she whispered.

Her friend lifted her head from their conspiratorial conversation. "Hello? Anyone here?"

Sounds of movement echoed from somewhere in the building, and a moment later, the tall man with thinning blond hair, despite his young age, appeared. Tom immediately smiled, sending a fresh wave of anxiety rolling through Opal. "Hi, ladies. What can I help you with?"

Penelope pulled the coffee cup from Opal's tight grip and held it out to Tom. "We were just at Malcolm's quick service counter for coffee, and for some crazy reason, the barista thought we'd ordered three coffees to go instead of two. She gave us the third one on the house, and since we were headed in your direction, we decided to give it to you."

Tom's countenance brightened. "That's awfully nice of you."

Penelope's smile grew bigger, and she set the coffee on the counter. "I hope you don't mind sugar and cream."

He slid the coffee toward him. "Just how I like it."

He lifted it, and Opal held her breath while he took a sip. He made no outward indication of the taste and set the cup down. "How can I help you ladies today?"

Penelope nudged Opal with her shoe.

Opal donned a relaxed smile. "Marla is thinking about switching up the personal items she offers at the inn to something more spa-like. I told her I'd look into it for her."

Tom chuckled. "Excellent. Free coffee and a possible increase in sales. A guy can't complain about that. Step this way, and I'll let you check out our samples. You can take some back to Marla if you'd like."

Tom picked up his coffee and headed into a back room. Penelope grinned at her, and Opal closed her eyes for a brief second, praying that everything would go according to plan. Perhaps she wasn't cut out for witchcraft after all.

They entered what appeared to be a stockroom, and Tom took another drink before he set down his coffee and slid a box from a nearby shelf. He set the box in the center of a small, square table that had well-worn folding chairs around it. "This has all my spa samples in it. You can open them, sniff, try them, whatever you like."

Opal and Penelope sat next to each other, and Penelope began pulling small bottles of shampoo and lotion from the box and placing them on the table, categorizing them by type. Opal pulled out a stack of wrapped soaps. "Can we open these?"

Tom grabbed a thick white binder with warped edges and sat opposite Opal. "Absolutely. There's a sink in the bathroom next door if you want to see how they lather. Or, if you decide on a few lines that you like, I'll send you home with a complete set of samples. You can demo them with Marla."

Penelope grinned. "I love samples."

Opal shot her a look, reminding her they were there on business, witchy and otherwise, and shouldn't be goofing around.

Penelope opened a brown bottle with green leaves spiraling up the side and sniffed. "Oh, gosh. This smells amazing."

She held the bottle toward Opal. "Try it."

Opal took a small sniff and then immediately drew a larger breath, filling her lungs with the amazing scent. "Citrus and..."

"Raspberry tangerine," Tom said before she could read the bottle.

Opal smiled. "It's absolutely delightful."

"Good," he responded. "I'll make sure you take some home."

Penelope sniffed another and then scrunched her nose. "That is a definite no."

One thing Opal could say was that she appreciated her friend's taste, and therefore, wouldn't need to bother smelling that one.

Tom tilted back his cup, indicating he'd drank a good portion of coffee, and Opal wondered if the spell had kicked in yet. Despite her reluctance to perform it in the first place, she was eager to see if her skills had worked.

Opal planned her sentence to be as non-confrontational as possible before she spoke. "I guess you'll be doing a lot more hotel hospitality business now that Jason's gone."

His features morphed into a look of concern. "Yeah. I hate to say it, but his loss is my gain. He doesn't have anyone to take over for him, so it looks like I'm sitting pretty."

He frowned and glanced between her and Penelope. "I apologize. That came out a lot ruder than it should have. I'm deeply sorry for his family's loss. Kandace has already gone through a lot where Jason was concerned. A beautiful woman like her doesn't need more heartache."

Opal wanted to correct him and say that no woman, regardless of her looks, deserved heartache. At least she knew the spell was having an effect. A puff of pride coursed through her, encouraging her to continue while she had the chance. "Do you know Kandace well?"

He snorted. "I'd say so. We've—"

He stopped abruptly and shook his head. "Did the barista add a few shots of espresso to that coffee? I swear my tongue is going faster than my mind."

Both women laughed awkwardly.

"I don't think so," Penelope answered. "Sorry."

He waved away her apology. "Not a biggie. A strong shot of caffeine will help me power through the day. If tonight is anything like last night, Kandace won't let me get much sleep."

Tom opened the binder, seemingly unaware of his reveal. He flipped open the clips and removed a sheet of paper. "This has our prices for all products."

He circled a section of typing. "These are what Marla purchases right now. You can see the raspberry tangerine scent is in the next highest quality section. It shouldn't subtract much from her bottom line."

Opal nodded, pleased. She truly did think upgrading would be a nice touch to the old house's charm. "That's wonderful."

"Oh," Penelope exclaimed. "Smell this one."

Opal inhaled a delightfully fresh ocean scent. "That one is really nice. I would think both men and women would appreciate it."

"Absolutely," Tom agreed. "It's one of my top sellers here along the coast. Reminds folks about the beauty they have waiting right outside."

Opal nodded and slid a sideways glance toward Tom. "I stopped by Bonnie's a few days ago. She and Sally were a wreck."

"I can only imagine," Tom said.

As far as Opal could tell, she couldn't detect any deception in Tom's words or actions, but he might be good at hiding things.

Penelope caught her gaze and gave a slight nod, encouraging her to continue.

Opal released a slow breath. So far, so good. "I was hoping she knew the date of the funeral, but I guess it was too soon. You haven't heard anything, have you?"

He shook his head. "Nope, not a word. I suppose someone will let us know shortly."

That didn't get her any new information.

Penelope turned to him. "It's all so sad. I wish I knew what happened to Jason. Do you think it's suicide or possibly murder?"

"Murder," he said without thinking.

Then he blinked in confusion several times and glanced quickly between the two of them. "Just my opinion."

Opal waved away his concern. "Of course. We're only talking speculation. I actually think someone murdered him, too."

The phone rang, and Opal panicked. Her time was up.

Tom stood and answered a wall phone. "Hang on just a moment, Terry, and I'll be right with you."

He pushed a button to put the call on hold and hung up the phone. His gaze shifted to Opal. "Any other questions I can answer right now?"

She started to shake her head and then stopped. "Okay, there is one, and it has nothing to do with supplies. Penelope and I were discussing it on the way over, and I'm curious how others would answer."

He lifted his chin in response. "Shoot."

Opal steeled her nerves. "If you had the opportunity to kill someone you really hated, would you? Say someone like Jason who competed with your business? Could you kill him?"

He met her gaze head on. "Nope."

Opal frowned. "Shouldn't you ponder the idea first?"

"No ma'am. Killing is not in my blood. Not spiders or flies, and certainly not people or pets. Goes against everything I believe in."

Opal believed he was telling the truth. The knowledge that she hadn't been sitting in the presence of a murderer and the fact that he hadn't taken offense to her questions brought her great relief. "I feel the same. Life is precious."

"Agreed," Penelope added.

Tom nodded toward the boxes. "Take whatever you want out of those along with the price list. I'll check in with you and Marla in a few days to see what you think."

She suddenly liked Tom a whole lot better than before. "Thanks. That sounds fantastic."

After he left the backroom, she and Penelope gathered samples. Opal took the ones she thought might be good ideas, and Penelope piled up most of the rest.

Opal trapped her with a questioning look. "Seriously?"

Penelope shrugged. "He said to take what we wanted. These all smell so good, and I can't decide."

Opal rolled her eyes and headed toward the door. Tom sat at the front desk, holding the receiver to his ear.

"You know, Terry," he said. "You haven't asked for a discount, but I'm making a fortune off you. I really ought to give you a deeper price break."

Tom pulled the receiver away and looked at it. He gave a small shake of his head as though confused.

Opal inadvertently caught his attention as they passed, and she waved as though she hadn't just caused the poor man to take a hit to his bottom line. He smiled in return, unaware of what she'd done, and she and Penelope strode out the door.

Once they were back in Penelope's car, her friend released a crazed laugh. "Oh, my stars. I can't believe we pulled it off, Opal. I almost had a heart attack when you flat out asked him."

Opal filled her lungs and blew out a breath. "I can't believe it either. We must be crazy."

"Oh, no," Penelope said and laughed. "This is only the first of the Crystal Cove Capers. We're going to be solving crimes left and right before you know it."

Opal placed a hand over her chest. "I'm not sure my heart can take it."

Penelope started the engine and smiled at her. "Just wait. You'll see."

CHAPTER TWENTY-TWO

Jason Conrad's funeral ended up being exactly one week after Opal had found him floating in the river. On one hand, Opal didn't favor the idea of attending a funeral with all the overwhelming emotions. On the other hand, she wouldn't miss this one for the world. She'd likely have all her suspects in one place.

She dressed in the least witchy black dress she had, one probably shorter than was acceptable at a funeral, but the rest of her choices with their flowing skirts and bells sewn along the hem might cause some speculation.

She met her grandfather downstairs in the living room of the old Victorian cottage and didn't blink an eye when she found Eleanor sitting next to him on the blue velvet couch, both looking at the same magazine.

John glanced up after a second. "Ready?"

Opal nodded, and the three of them headed toward the front door.

Familiar blustery weather awaited them. The atmosphere swirled with heavy energy that seemed appropriate for the sad day. Despite the fact that none of her party had been particularly close to Jason, Crystal Cove was a small town, and when members of the community hurt, everyone mourned with them.

The somber day reminded Opal that the universe could cut a life short at any time, and because she didn't know how much time she'd have with her grandfather, she chose to ride with him and Eleanor as opposed to driving herself. No one spoke during the short distance to the church, and Opal allowed her grandpa to open the door for her after he did for Eleanor.

The small white church with a gray-roofed spire had sat high on the hill for the past hundred years. The property looked out over the tops of the houses to the wild ocean beyond. As much as Opal needed to be where she was, she longed to have the sea breeze caress her skin and the sounds of the waves drown out the voices in her head.

Instead, she resigned herself for what lay ahead.

Together, the three of them entered through the double doors of the church and proceeded to the chapel where everyone had gathered. Opal, John and Eleanor offered more condolences to Bonnie, and then her grandfather and Eleanor walked off to claim seats at the back of the chapel.

Opal looked around for Bonnie's daughter who should have been by her side but was noticeably missing. The fact that Bonnie stood sentry alone next to Jason's casket bothered Opal. "Where's Sally?"

A pained expression blanched Bonnie's face. "She said she'd be here, but I'm starting to wonder," she said in a quiet voice. "Sally and Jason never did have a good relationship, but I thought she'd put that aside if only for today."

Opal raised her brows. "Oh, goodness. Maybe this has been too much for her. It would be for anyone. I'd be happy to head over to your house and help her if she needs it."

Tears sprang to Bonnie's eyes, and she shook her head. "No. I'm not going to force her to attend her brother's funeral if she doesn't want to. I tried to make them get along in life, and they didn't. What's the point now?"

Opal nodded, hoping she could somehow reassure Bonnie that everything would be okay. "Is it all right if I stay with you then? Unless she shows?"

Bonnie shot her a grateful look. "Thank you, but my sisters will be here shortly."

Opal offered her a kind smile. "Well, I'll just stick around until they do, okay?"

The older woman took Opal's hand and squeezed. "Thank you."

Opal remained by her side until two plump ladies, with eyes similar to Bonnie's, arrived ten minutes before the service began. Opal hugged Bonnie and made her way to the bench where her grandfather waited. He and Eleanor scooted to make room for her.

Across the church, Ryan caught her attention and waved with an elated grin on his face. Opal awkwardly lifted a hand and returned the gesture. Then she quickly turned away, only to notice Lucas watching her from the other side of the chapel.

Son of a sea turtle. This was so not happening.

She'd never gotten any vibes from Lucas in the past, but she swore his unhappiness barreled toward her like a rogue wave.

She huffed her frustration, drawing a look from her grandfather.

Fine.

She wouldn't look at either of the men. Their problems were not hers.

Instead, she directed her gaze forward and focused on the podium ahead to wait for the priest to begin.

Five minutes into the service, during a somber hymn, a commotion behind Opal drew her gaze. Kandace strode down the aisle wearing all black, including a huge hat and veil, with her arm firmly latched around Tom's. Kandace's mother held little Beau's hand and followed behind.

People in the row ahead of Opal scooted to make room for the foursome. After the song ended, the priest addressed Kandace. "There are plenty of seats at the front for family."

Kandace lifted her chin. "I'm aware of that, but we're quite fine here."

Opal caught her grandfather's gaze, and he lifted his brows in disappointed surprise.

As far as Opal noticed, Kandace didn't turn her gaze from the podium once. Unfortunately, Ryan sat in the same line of sight, so every time she checked on Jason's ex-wife, she found Ryan smiling at her.

Then, of course, she couldn't resist glancing to see if Lucas had noticed, and every dang time, he was watching her, too.

She had to say something to Lucas, had to let him know there was nothing between her and Ryan, if for no other reason than to distance herself from the man who'd broken her heart.

Also, she'd likely see Lucas regularly at the police station, and he was a potential source of information, though he hadn't given her much so far. Still, she'd rather keep them on a friendly basis. If he believed she'd lied to him about Ryan, that would be hard to do.

During the service, Beau bounced from lap to lap, not content to sit still. His mother seemed to have all the patience in the world for him, but he didn't want to stay on her lap. He wiggled and squirmed until she set him on the floor to play.

He stayed quiet for several minutes but then pushed past her to where he could reach Tom. Beau patted his leg for attention. "Daddy. Daddy, see this?"

Daddy?

Opal turned her complete focus to the supposedly bereaved family in front of her.

Beau shoved a small red fire truck in Tom's direction. Tom spoke to him quietly and lifted him to his lap so that Beau could show off the toy.

Daddy? The word echoed in her mind again.

Tom was most definitely not Beau's daddy. Well, at least not that Opal knew of. In addition to that, Kandace and Jason hadn't been divorced long enough for Beau to start calling another man daddy. Not in her opinion, anyway.

Unless Kandace and Tom's relationship had been going on longer than anyone knew, and little Beau had come to think of Tom as a father.

Either way, having Jason out of the picture sure made Kandace's life easier.

The second the service ended, Opal said goodbye to her grandfather and Eleanor, letting them know she'd be headed to work and would find a ride home later. They left, and Opal turned, searching out Lucas.

She spotted him hugging Bonnie, and then he turned toward a side exit of the chapel. She hustled after him.

Outside, she found him closing in on his police SUV.

"Lucas," she called.

He turned in her direction, and she caught a look of edginess cross his face. Part of her wanted to turn back, but the other part needed him to hear a few things first.

She offered a smile as she approached. "Hey, do you have a minute?"

He made a point of looking at his watch. "Only one. I'm on duty."

His aura was darker than normal, and she cursed the fact that she couldn't get an honest read from him.

With them only feet apart, her nerves gave way, and she couldn't bring herself to talk about Ryan. "I wanted to mention a couple of things about Jason's case that you might not be aware of."

Apparently, her words held enough intrigue because he gave her his full attention. "Tell me."

She stepped closer to eliminate some of the space between them. "I'm sure you noticed, as we all did, that Kandace arrived with Tom."

He dipped his head. "Yeah. Renewed rumors about the two of them have been circulating. I guess after she admitted their relationship in a police interview, she decided she had no reason to hide it any longer."

"Do you know why she hid it in the first place? She was a single woman, free to date."

He turned his gaze to look across the parking lot to the ocean in the distance. "Yeah. Not sure why she hid it. Unless, like you said, it started well before she and Jason had separated."

Opal nodded. "That's what I've heard, too."

He turned and rested an elbow on his car. Deep green eyes bored into hers. "Truth is, they weren't divorced yet. Jason refused to sign the papers."

Opal's stomach turned. "Wait...seriously?"

He lifted his chin in an affirmative response.

She wasn't about to ask why he chose to share that information with her. Perhaps he didn't consider it confidential. "During the service, Beau called Tom *daddy*. Do you think he really could be?"

Lucas shook his head. "Nah. I don't think so. Beau is almost three, and it's only been recently that Kandace and Jason's relationship went downhill."

"That you know of," she added.

He studied her face, and she wished she could read his thoughts. "It's true. We always think we know what someone is thinking until we discover otherwise."

She drew her brows together. Was he talking about her? "Did you notice Sally wasn't there?"

He nodded. "I found it peculiar, but I try not to judge how others handle death."

She'd always tried to do the same. Grief was such a personal experience. "Bonnie said Sally and Jason had never gotten along. Still, a sister would take the opportunity to say goodbye to her brother, wouldn't she...unless she had another reason to not go."

He shifted his stance. "You mean if perhaps she'd killed him?"

Opal shrugged. "I don't know if I think she could do it, but she has a lot of darkness in her soul. I can't help but wonder."

He remained silent for several moments though he kept his gaze on her. "I take it you can somehow sense darkness in others?"

The casual way he mentioned her abilities caught her off guard. His statement seemed to suggest that he accepted her unique qualities and that she might not need to defend them. "I can. People have auras that give me hints on their personalities and what might be going on inside them. Hers was especially dark."

He nodded. "Interesting. What does mine say?"

His curiosity warmed her, and she smiled. He didn't seem to know his was also dark, yet not in the same way as Sally's. "I don't know yet. Usually, I can get a reading right away, but yours is more obscure."

He chuckled. "Like maybe I'm hiding something?"

Her smile grew bigger. "Not necessarily. Sometimes I just need to get to know a person better before I can read him."

He studied her face, and a spark of their connection jumped between them. "Is that so?"

The sound of her name rode the breeze, and she looked back toward the church. Ryan waved as he hurried straight toward them.

"Oh, great," she groaned.

All traces of magic between her and Lucas disappeared. He cleared his throat. "Looks like your boyfriend has caught you with another guy. Hope he's not too upset."

She lifted her brows in surprise. "What? No. Oh, no. There is most definitely nothing between Ryan and me."

He lifted a shoulder and let it drop in a nonchalant manner. "I saw you two at the beach. You looked pretty cozy to me."

"If that's what you thought, you would be dead wrong. He'd hurt himself, and I was just helping him to the boardwalk because he was unsteady."

"Opal," Ryan said, sounding a little out of breath as he reached them. No doubt because he'd sprinted across the parking lot like a boy chasing a puppy. "There you are. I was looking for you everywhere."

Lucas turned to her with a raised brow that said her statement didn't match Ryan's actions.

She folded her arms and turned to Ryan with a bland stare. "Did you need something?"

"You," he said brightly. "I need you, my angel."

Lucas coughed, and Opal's world hovered on the edge of sanity. "I'm sorry. I was just headed to work. I don't really have time to chat now."

Ryan's face brightened. "Let me give you a ride."

She recognized the look in his eyes, the same handsome one that used to give her butterflies of excitement.

Her stomach twisted, and she glanced between the two men. "Actually, Officer Keller was going to drive me. I have a few things I need to discuss with him."

Ryan flicked a quick glance at Lucas, seeming as though he'd barely realized they had company. His expression turned wary. "You know Opal?"

Lucas drew his brows together in confusion. "What kind of question is that?"

Ryan puffed out his chest. "An important one."

Lucas turned to her and narrowed his gaze as though he knew something wasn't right and suspected she might have something to do with it.

She flashed Lucas an innocent smile. "Are you ready then? I really shouldn't be late for work."

She hurried to the passenger side, climbed in, and shut the door on the potential problem brewing outside. The two men spoke and then suddenly Ryan's mouth split into a wide grin again. Lucas nodded to him and then climbed into his SUV, shutting the door between them and a grinning, idiotic man.

Blessed Gaia, what had she done? She wasn't entirely sure that the current Ryan was better than the old.

At least he couldn't open his big mouth. She needed to remember that.

Lucas started the engine and pulled from his parking space. "What's up with Ryan? I've never seen him that odd."

She swallowed her guilt. "I'm not sure. He was a little weird the day I helped him from the beach. I think he might have hit his head."

"What makes you think that? Was he bleeding?"

"No."

"A big lump then?"

She had to remember she was dealing with a trained police officer and to choose her words carefully. "Not that I noticed. But I didn't really check either."

"Then how did you know he needed help?"

She readjusted the seatbelt across her chest. "He said he did, and he seemed unsteady."

"But you didn't question him further as to what happened?"

She dared a glance at Lucas who stared at her for several seconds before he turned his attention back to the road.

She feared he could see right through her, and she struggled for a proper explanation. "If he wouldn't have been considerably better by the time we reached the boardwalk, I would have taken him to the clinic."

And that was the truth. Though she didn't know how she would have explained his situation.

"Hmm... I guess he's okay then. Just seems a little goofy and awfully infatuated with you."

Apparently, that was her karma for completing a selfish spell.

"I don't know why," she answered. "It's not like I'm nice to him."

He chuckled. "Ain't that the truth. Are you nice to any guys?"

She turned to him, insulted. "I'm nice to you. Especially considering the fact that you gave me a ticket the first time we met."

He tilted his head toward her in agreement. "There is that."

Lucas remained quiet until he came to a stop near the center of town. Then he met her gaze with intense eyes. "Let me buy you lunch."

His question was so simple and yet so complicated. "Today?"

"Sure. We could do it now. Brigid's Bistro is fairly new and a nice place. You might like to try it out."

She gave him a sad smile. "I really do have to be to work soon. I wasn't just saying it to get away from Ryan."

Lucas's expression dimmed. She didn't know if she should be relieved that she had a reason to decline or unhappy that she'd disappointed him again and quite possibly herself.

He gave her a curt nod. "Yeah. Sure. I understand."

From the look in his eye, she was certain he didn't believe her. "How about lunch tomorrow?" she asked.

Only Mother Earth knew why she'd opened her mouth. Eating together would only blur the boundaries between them.

The smile that lit his face warmed her heart. "Sounds great. I'll pick you up."

Except a lunch date with one of the guys might be a problem with her grandfather. "Um...I will actually be at the station in the morning, but I don't want to stir gossip. It's better for both of us. How about I meet you there?"

He parked in front of the Rosewood Inn and seemed about to argue but then nodded. "Deal. If I see you in the office earlier, I'll pretend I don't know you."

She chuckled and climbed out, thinking he was teasing her, but as he drove away, she wondered if he'd been serious.

CHAPTER TWENTY-THREE

The station was quiet the next morning with Irina off until noon and most of the on-duty officers out patrolling the beach or helping to pull a drunk driver's truck from a roadside ravine. Opal hadn't seen hide nor hair of Lucas, and her grandfather was behind closed doors in his office.

The chief had tasked her with answering the phones. Irina had left a note with strict instructions not to touch anything else. So many rules had made for two boring hours so far.

She'd cleaned the top of the desk and wiped down filing cabinets. Unfortunately, those duties hadn't taken any time at all. Irina had also left instructions not to turn on her computer, so Opal had taken to playing games on her phone to pass the time.

The station's phone finally rang, and she jumped. She straightened her back and lifted the receiver. "Crystal Cove Police Department. How may I help you?"

Dang if she didn't sound professional.

"Help. I need help!" A woman's voice shrieked across the line, sending panic straight to Opal's core.

The woman rambled so fast that Opal couldn't understand a word she said. "Ma'am. Calm down, ma'am, so that you can give me your information. What is your address?"

Opal glanced frantically around Irina's pristine desk for a pen and pad of paper. Nothing. She pulled open the nearest drawer and grabbed what she needed.

"This. Is. Carlene. Bateman," she said slowly with irritation dripping from each word.

Opal released a quiet sigh. Everything with Carlene was a crisis. "Carlene, this is Opal. What's your emergency?"

"Opal?" Her voice took on a completely different tone, sounding almost cheerful. "I'd heard you were back in town. How's your grandpa?"

She almost snorted a laugh. "He's good, but you said you need help. Tell me what's wrong, and I'll send someone right out."

"Oh." Back to the irritated voice. "It's that damned fool husband of mine. He was trying to back the truck into Lake Lytle and now the truck bed is half under water. That idiot man of mine thinks he can still drive it out, but I'm standing here on the edge of the bank, and it's sinking by the minute with the boat still tied to the trailer. I should just let the whole thing go down with him in it and walk away."

Opal almost believed the feisty woman might do it. "Can Harold swim, Carlene?"

"Yes," she answered with distaste coloring her words.

"Okay. Tell him to get out of the truck and that I have officers and a tow truck on the way."

"Get out of the truck, Harold!" Carlene hollered, forcing Opal to jerk the phone away from her ear. "I said, get out of the truck."

When it seemed safe to continue their conversation, Opal held the phone close again. "Is he getting out?"

"He's arguing, but he's doing it."

"Good."

Carlene chuckled. "Oops, there he goes into the water."

The woman was obviously enjoying the entertainment provided by her husband. Opal would bet that wouldn't go over well by the time Harold reached the bank.

"And he's fine?" Opal asked.

"He's fine."

Opal rolled her eyes. "I'm going to put you on hold while I contact officers and the tow truck."

The sound of shuffling behind Opal caught her attention, and she turned. Lucas approached the desk. "I can help you with that. What do you need?"

She quickly explained the situation and location of the emergency, and Lucas lifted the radio mike from his shoulder. She held his gaze while he assigned officers to the scene, impressed by how he took command of the situation.

When he finished, she turned her attention back to her caller. "Officers are on the way, Carlene. How's Harold?"

"He's here with me looking like he's about to bawl like a baby," she chortled.

"Shut up, Carlene." Harold's voice echoed in the background.

Yep, he was not a happy man. "Okay, then, Carlene. I'm going to hang up now. You should have help there in just a few minutes."

"All righty then, Opal. The truck and the boat are toast, but we're just fine. You make sure you stop by and say hello soon."

She tried to withhold a grin. "I'll be sure to do that. See you soon."

Opal hung up before Carlene could start another tirade. She looked upward to Lucas. "Did you send a tow truck, too?"

A twinkle lit in his eye. "It's all been taken care of."

She nodded her approval. "I have a feeling the Bateman household isn't going to be a happy place tonight."

He chuckled. "Is it ever?"

She laughed and shook her head.

He lifted his chin in acknowledgement. "We still on for lunch?" he asked quietly.

She started to answer, but her grandfather opened the door to his office and cut her off. She gave a quick nod before the cranky old man appeared.

John glanced between the two of them with suspicious eyes, and Opal turned away.

"Lucas? Glad it's you. Come take a look at this."

Officer Keller walked off without saying another word.

Second, third, and fourth thoughts rumbled through Opal's mind about agreeing to have lunch with Lucas. With a town as small as Crystal Cove, her grandfather would eventually hear something. Probably sooner than later. Still, she and Lucas were only friends, and therefore, in her opinion, there was no need to disclose anything to the chief.

Co-workers had lunch together all the time.

Her grandfather's door closed, cutting her off from overhearing anything interesting. She sighed and turned back to the drudgery, her ten minutes of excitement now gone.

Opal gathered the unneeded pen and notepad and placed them back in the drawer exactly where she'd found them. She wouldn't give Irina a reason to say she'd messed up her space.

Still, Opal had to admit that even though the morning had been boring, she much preferred answering phones to organizing her grandfather's desk. She closed Irina's drawer and then stared at the one beneath it. Curiosity struck hard.

Opal played volleyball with her conscience for all of three seconds before she slid open the second drawer. She wondered exactly what a woman like Irina might have inside.

At first glance, the contents appeared to be another exercise in boredom. A lint roller. A small plastic box full of girl necessities. A plastic spoon, and a cup of ramen noodles for an emergency lunch, Opal supposed.

Nothing terribly interesting.

She lifted the noodles to examine the carton for calorie and nutrition content. For the so-called health nut, the ramen noodles were a shocking find. So much for Irina not eating junk food. In her opinion, ramen noodles were far worse than donuts.

Opal made a mental note and filed that knowledge away in case it might come in handy for blackmail material at some point.

A photo that had been tucked between the noodles and the side of the drawer had fallen flat when she'd removed the container. Opal picked it up, enjoying the deliciousness of going through the snotty woman's drawers.

She flipped it over and widened her eyes.

The happy couple.

Jason, with less hair than Opal remembered, stood next to a smiling Irina, with his arm draped lazily across her shoulder. They were in wetsuits with the ocean at their backs. The angle of the photo looked as though Jason had taken it as a selfie.

She studied his expression, noting that he didn't seem as happy as Irina did. In contrast, the smile on her face pushed out her cheeks and lingered in her eyes. She obviously was happy to be with him on that particular day, but the feeling wasn't mutual.

Opal lowered the photo and pondered why they'd been on-again, off-again. Had Jason cheated on Irina like he'd supposedly done with Kandace? Once a cheater, always a cheater?

Had he finally paid the price for it?

Opal glanced at the photo again and gasped. She drew the picture closer to her face to study it better, and what she found slammed her like a sneaker wave.

There.

Right there, around Irina's neck, was the necklace Opal had found at the scene of the crime.

She smacked her palm on the desk. Bingo

Ryan and Irina must have struggled while she'd tried to end his life, and one of them had broken the necklace in the process. It all made sense.

Irina was the murderer, and Opal had solved the case.

She pushed back from Irina's desk and hurried to her grandfather's office. She knocked rapidly, not caring if she was interrupting.

Before either of them could have a chance to answer, she pushed open the door. "Grandpa. Lucas. You are not going to believe what I found."

Both had surprised looks on their faces as she approached and dropped the photo between them. "Look at the necklace Irina is wearing. It's the one I found at the crime scene."

Lucas glanced at the photo, but her grandfather shot her a disappointed look. "I already know about the necklace."

She blinked in surprise, and her excitement deflated into a week-old balloon. "You do?"

John took the picture and slid it into his desk. "Yes. Irina informed me of it a few days after Jason's death when she happened to see a photo of the evidence."

This news sent Opal's thoughts spiraling. "What did she say about it? Did she admit to being with Jason before he died? Were they fighting?"

Her grandfather held up a hand to stop her. "The necklace isn't one of a kind, Opal. Apparently, he also gave one to Kandace a couple of years ago."

She glanced between Lucas and the police chief. "Okay, then. That's easy. Which of them no longer has hers? That should lead us straight to our prime suspect."

"*My* prime suspect," her grandfather countered. "And no, it doesn't. Neither of the women can produce their necklaces."

Opal slumped her shoulders. She was the world's biggest idiot.

John chastised her with a look. "We've done our job, Opal, and we don't require your help. Sorry."

She looked to Lucas who commiserated with a half-hearted smile.

Opal nodded in defeat. "Sorry for busting in. I'll just be outside."

Her grandfather cleared his throat before she reached the office door. "Why don't you head out for an early lunch? It's not long before Irina returns, and you've done enough for the day."

By "done enough", she was sure he hadn't meant in a helpful way. More like made a big enough fool of herself. "Sure thing. I'll see you later then. Bye, Lucas."

As she closed the door, she heard Lucas speak. Instead of going back to her desk, she stayed to listen.

"Hey John, if we're done here, I think I'll head out in a few to get something to eat, too. Mighty hungry today. Want me to bring anything back?"

"Nah, I'm good," her grandfather responded. "Leave the door open so I can hear the phone, and make sure Opal's gone before you go. We don't need her snooping in anything else."

Her heart cracked and pain widened it. Not only did her grandfather think she was an idiot, but he didn't want her anywhere on the premises.

She blinked back tears as she hurried to grab her purse and get out the door before Lucas saw her. She wished she could bail on lunch, but that would mean she'd admitted defeat twice in one day.

She couldn't let Lucas or anyone know she'd heard what her grandfather had said. Not even Penelope. At least not yet.

She needed to lick her wounds first.

CHAPTER TWENTY-FOUR

By the time Opal had parked near Brigid's Bistro and exited her car, she'd managed to compose herself. She'd driven down a side street and stopped on the way so that she could fix the mascara her tears had messed up. In the process, she'd realized her grandfather could only make her feel stupid if she allowed it. Discovering that photo with Irina wearing the necklace was a good find. A great one.

She was sure many detectives found clues that led to nowhere. That didn't mean they were incompetent. It only meant they were doing their jobs.

As she approached the restaurant, she caught sight of Lucas watching her from one of the outdoor tables located beneath a black and maroon awning. Her first thought was that their chances of someone seeing them together would increase a hundred-fold if they sat outside.

At least the restaurant had placed several ficus trees between them and Main Street to give the illusion of privacy. Perhaps she could hide behind one.

On second thought, all it would take was one local sitting inside or one of the workers to ignite the gossip chain. Fact was, she was having lunch with Lucas and everyone would know. She had to be okay with that.

And she was.

Their gazes met, and his lips turned upward in what some would call a devastating smile.

They'd shared smiles before, but she was certain she hadn't seen this one.

His expression unleashed tingles inside her and left her off-balance.

She gave him a small wave and then headed inside the restaurant. The hostess, someone Opal didn't know, led her to Lucas's table.

He stood as they approached.

Opal sent the hostess a nod of thanks and allowed Lucas to slide out her chair for her.

"Fancy meeting you here," he said as he resumed his seat.

"Such a coincidence," she responded.

He grinned and then his expression sobered. "I don't think I've seen the chief be that tough on anyone before."

She rolled her eyes in an attempt to keep the pain at bay. "It seems that's a special treat he saves just for me."

He lifted a brow. "Things always like this between you?"

She snorted. "No. We had a great relationship before I left for school."

"I wonder what's set him off now, then?"

Their waitress appeared. She dropped off a bread-basket, filled their glasses with water, and left with their order.

Opal waited until they were alone to answer. "I'm not entirely sure, but I don't think he likes me in his business."

One side of Lucas's mouth tilted up. "But police business is something you enjoy."

He didn't even bother to phrase it as a question, which she appreciated. "I do. I like seeing wrongs righted. Why is that such a bad thing?"

"I don't think it is, Opal. I think good should win over evil, too."

She took a sip of water and then sighed. "I guess I need to learn how to navigate him better."

He chuckled. "Marching into his office and announcing you've found the killer might be a little over the top."

Heat spread across her cheeks, and she shrugged to cover her embarrassment. "Are you positive Irina isn't guilty?"

Police chatter came across his shoulder radio, and he turned it down. "I'm not one hundred percent sure, no. But she did love the guy. I don't doubt that she's crushed by his death."

Opal released a frustrated sigh and picked up a crusty roll. "Then where does that leave us?"

Instead of answering, Lucas lifted his chin, gesturing toward the sidewalk.

Opal turned her gaze just as Kandace, Vicky and Beau strolled past them. She widened her eyes and shifted her gaze back to Lucas. "Kandace? Is she your number one suspect?"

She expected him to tell her to mind her business, but instead, his irises darkened, and he nodded. "She stands to make bank with the life insurance policy. She's already spending it. New clothes and a new car, and she doesn't even have the money yet."

Opal leaned forward, grateful for the bone he'd tossed her. "She bought a new car?"

"Cute little sporty red thing."

Opal loved nice cars, too. In fact, she'd used some of her trust fund money to purchase her Mustang.

The sound of a small child's voice cut through the atmosphere, and Opal turned to look inside the restaurant. "Speak of the devil," she whispered.

Lucas's gaze intensified. "Excuse me?"

"They're coming in here," she said quietly. "Kandace and crew."

When he turned to look, she placed a hand on his forearm. "Turn around. Don't let them catch you staring."

He relaxed his shoulders and did as she asked. "You plan on spying on them here?"

"Yes." She answered in a manner that suggested he was crazy if he didn't think she would. "Any chance for information is a good thing."

Twinges of guilt for ignoring Lucas on their lunch date pricked Opal over the next ten minutes while she strained to hear Kandace's and Vicky's conversation. When Kandace confessed to her mother that she was glad Jason was dead, ire rose inside Opal, and she turned to Lucas.

"I cannot believe Kandace's nerve," she said in a hushed whisper. "She just told her mom she's happy Jason is gone. That things have worked out well for her."

Lucas drew his brows together. "How did you hear all that?"

Opal lifted her shoulders in an innocent shrug. "Can't you hear them?"

"Bits and pieces, but not everything you heard."

She shot a nasty glare in Kandace's direction. "You should take her in for questioning."

He chuckled and shook his head. "Doesn't work like that. But don't worry. We have her in our sights."

That wasn't good enough for Opal. Crystal Cove had a murderer gloating in their midst, and she couldn't let that happen. She stood.

Alarm flashed in Lucas's eyes. "What are you doing?"

"If you're not going to question Kandace, then I will."

"You can't do that."

She squared her shoulders. "Watch me."

Opal strode straight for Kandace and crew, stopping when she reached their table. The bright lemon-yellow of Kandace's aura hinted at her fear of losing control. Made perfect sense for someone trying to hang on to an illusion of innocence and disguise her guilt.

Kandace glanced up with curiosity in her gaze. "Yes?"

The full fury of injustice rose inside Opal. "You disgust me."

Kandace's face blanched. "What did you say?"

Opal inhaled a deep breath and prepared to give the woman all she had. "You're walking all over town, celebrating the fact that your husband is dead."

"Ex-husband," Kandace corrected with a sneer in her voice.

Opal smirked. "Is that right?"

Kandace dropped her jaw, and Opal headed straight for the jugular. "Would you care to tell me why Jason's son is already calling another man 'Daddy'? It's a little soon for that, isn't it? Unless, of course, you've been planning Jason's death all along. No need to hide that from little Beau because he won't remember his real daddy, anyway. Am I getting close?"

Kandace stood so fast that her chair fell backward. Red stained her cheeks, and fire burned in her eyes. "You have no idea what you're talking about. Best that you shut that trap of yours and get out of here, now. Just because you're the chief's daughter doesn't mean I can't sue you for slander."

Opal shook her head, not buying into Kandace's threats. "You might as well confess. It's only a matter of time before the police piece together enough evidence to arrest you."

Anger distorted Kandace's features. "Go ahead and try to prove I killed him. I dare you."

Opal lifted defiant brows. "Might not turn out so well for you. An ex-husband who wasn't an ex yet. A lover who was your husband's rival."

People seated nearby gasped and began to whisper.

Kandace gripped her hands into fists, and her aura vibrated with fury.

Opal didn't care. She wanted to push her until she broke. "A new relationship where your little boy thinks Tom is his daddy. Is he Kandace? Is Tom Beau's daddy?"

Kandace took a step closer to Opal. "I don't have to listen to this."

But Opal was on a roll.

Vicky grabbed Beau and stepped around Opal to walk back inside the restaurant. Kandace tried to follow, but Lucas stood and blocked her way.

"A fat insurance policy," Opal added. "I found the necklace Jason gave you at the scene of the crime. It's all starting to add up."

Kandace shook her head, her blond hair swinging from side to side. "All you have is circumstantial evidence. You can't prove anything."

Lucas's lips curved into a self-confident smile. "We've convicted felons on much less evidence than that."

Rage exploded on Kandace's face, and she swung a fist at Opal. Lucas pushed her out of the way, and Kandace's punch landed squarely on the side of his mouth.

He shook his head slowly and lifted two fingers to his lips. Opal winced when he came away with blood.

"Kandace Conrad, I'm placing you under arrest for assaulting an officer."

He grabbed one of her arms, but she yanked it free. She stared at Lucas for a fierce moment. Then, she vaulted the short wrought-iron fence, high heels and all, and raced off.

Lucas chased after and was on her in an instant, trapping her with muscled arms. She fought and almost brought them to the ground.

"Get off me," she screamed. "You can't do this."

Vicky, with Beau in her arms, emerged from the restaurant and jogged past Opal toward the two. Opal hurried over the fence, prepared to intervene if Vicky got in the way.

Lucas was less gentle with Kandace this time and quickly slapped handcuffs on her wrists. "You're under arrest Kandace Conrad. We'll start with assaulting an officer. You have the right to an attorney. If you can't afford one, one will be provided for you. Do you understand these rights?"

Tears streamed down Kandace's face, leaving trails of mascara in their wake. "No. I don't understand. You can't do this. What about my little boy?"

"Should have thought of that first," he said, sounding every bit the authoritative cop.

Lucas scanned the crowd until he caught Opal's gaze. "Sorry," he mouthed.

She shook her head, not sure why he was apologizing when she'd been the one to ruin their lunch date by going after Kandace.

Honestly, she couldn't believe everything had gone down as it had.

Lucas turned the crying Kandace in the direction of his police unit and marched her down the street for the whole town to see.

Vicky shot Opal a frantic glance and dropped a bawling Beau at Opal's feet. "This isn't right."

She raced after the officer and her cuffed daughter. "You can't do this, Lucas. It's not right."

Opal picked up the little boy and tried to comfort him. Poor thing would now have no mother or father if Opal's suspicions proved to be correct.

Lucas ignored the ranting older woman as he opened the backdoor of his SUV.

A blood-curdling scream exploded from Vicky's lungs, and all of Main Street paused. "*I said, no!* She didn't do it. You can't take her from my grandson. He needs his mother."

Lucas offered her a consoling look. "I'm sorry, Vicky."

"No." She shook her head frantically. "You don't understand. She didn't do it, because I did."

A roar of voices filled the void, and Opal clamped her free hand over her mouth in surprise.

Vicky had murdered Jason?

It took Opal a moment to realize she'd solved the case. Or at least she'd started events that had led to Vicky's confession.

She blinked as she took it all in. Wait until her grandfather heard about that. He'd have to give her credit now.

Vicky traded places with Kandace, and not long after Lucas had placed her mother in the back of the SUV, Kandace came to claim her son.

She pulled little Beau from Opal's arms. "I hate you," she said through gritted teeth.

Opal met her gaze head on. "I'm sorry, but this is your mother's to own. Not mine. Karma will always win."

Kandace glared and then stormed off.

Opal stood for a moment and then smiled. She supposed that working for the police department also meant that not everyone would be happy with her all the time. Surprisingly, she didn't mind taking the bad as long as she could do good.

EPILOGUE

When the cloud cover was thick over Crystal Cove, dusk came early. Only traces of light remained as Opal set out from the police station to walk the several blocks home. She'd endured a long day after Vicky's arrest and had decided the fresh air would do her good.

She needed time to process the day's events. She'd given verbal and written statements to her grandfather about everything that had transpired. And yes, she hadn't failed to notice his look of disapproval when she told him she'd been with Lucas when everything had gone down.

But she'd tried to lighten the mood by telling him they were only friends who'd happened to be eating lunch at the same place. It was true and all her grandfather needed to know.

Headlights came from behind, casting a long shadow ahead of her on the sidewalk. Instead of passing her, the car slowed, and she shot a nervous glance over her shoulder.

Lucas stopped his SUV next to her and lowered the window. "Hey."

A smile blossomed on her lips. Despite their shaky beginnings, they had worked amazingly well together that day. "I didn't jaywalk, did I?"

He grinned. "How about a ride?"

She lifted a teasing brow. "With a strange man?"

He shifted the SUV into park and exited his vehicle. He crossed behind it and stepped up onto the sidewalk next to her. Laughter danced in his eyes. "I'm sure I could find a reason to arrest you if you resist."

She folded her arms. "Is that so?"

He stepped closer, forcing her to look up to see him. "You know it is."

She laughed and held up her hands in defeat. "Okay, officer. I give up."

He opened the door for her, and electricity crackled between them as she climbed inside.

Instead of taking her straight home, he drove the short stretch to the outskirts of town, where an outcropping of rock overlooked the ocean, and parked. He rolled down the windows and cool, fresh air rushed in and surrounded them. In the distance, she could spot whitecaps as they rose above the ocean, only to disappear again.

Lucas turned to her. "This okay?"

She lifted a teasing brow. "You're going to ask now that we're here?"

He paused for a moment and then grinned. "Nah. You're my prisoner for the moment. You'll just have to enjoy the beautiful night."

She didn't know how to respond, so she only smiled.

"You know your grandfather is taking full credit for everything."

She dropped her jaw. "Full credit? He didn't even mention us?"

He chuckled. "Well, in a way. At one point, he did say he and the department solved the crime. I guess that includes us. But since Vicky gave the full details of the murder during his interrogation, he thinks he cracked the case."

Opal rolled her eyes. "I'm not even a paid member of the department. The least he can do is give me a little credit."

Lucas's expression sobered. "I think it's all part of the ruse to keep up a good front."

She exhaled and let her frustrations go. Despite him being a big pain in the butt, she would forever have a soft spot for him. "Because he's worried about looking bad."

Lucas nodded. "He's slowed down some lately. Not quite as sharp as he used to be. The only problem is the drive is still there, you know? And people don't want to break his heart, so they keep voting him in."

Her heart ached for her grandfather. "Which is why they hired you."

"Yeah," he said softly. "I'm not arguing the point that your grandfather does have invaluable insight and experience. He's had a remarkable career, and he's still an asset to the department."

She supposed that much was true. "Did you get a chance to read Vicky's confession? I'm dying to know how she got him into the river. It's not easy to move dead weight."

"Succinylcholine. Commonly called Sux."

She drew her brows together. "Never heard of it."

"When injected, it causes all muscles in the body to be paralyzed. Vicky lured Jason to the river with a promise to give him information on Tom that would likely cause Kandace to drop him. Big mistake on his part. Apparently, Jason hadn't signed the divorce papers because he was still hoping for a reconciliation."

"Don't tell me that. I don't want to feel sorry for Irina."

He gave a soft chuckle. "She's not that bad."

She slid him a sideways glance. "Says you."

"Anyway, after that, Vicky somehow found the strength to drag Jason the short distance to the river and push him in."

"Wow. I can't imagine how much hate a person would have to feel to do something like that."

"Yeah," Lucas agreed. "She believed she was doing it to save her daughter and grandson years of misery."

They both fell into silence. Opal replayed different aspects of the case, and then flicked her gaze to Lucas. "What about the necklace I found? Was it relevant? Did Vicky have it?"

Lucas shrugged. "She didn't own up to it. Some have speculated that Jason might have had it in his pocket and dropped it."

"Hmm..." She supposed that could have happened.

Opal closed her eyes and inhaled the invigorating air. She loved that Lucas somehow knew this was exactly what she needed and that he didn't treat her differently because she was a witch, as if her heritage was something foreign to fear like Ryan had done years ago.

"You're tired," he said. "I should get you home before you conk out on me."

She opened sleepy eyes. "I suppose. It has been a long day."

"It has. But Bonnie has closure now."

Opal was grateful for that. "I hope she can find a way to forgive her daughter for her behavior and have a decent relationship with her."

"Yeah."

He pinned her with his gaze for several seconds and smiled. Then he broke the moment and reached for the keys. He turned the ignition. As the engine jumped to life, a soft, echoing song came through her window and drove deep into her heart. She only heard it for a second before the sound of the engine drowned out whatever had been on the air.

She twisted her gaze to him. "Did you hear that?"

He shook his head. "What?"

She insisted he turn off the engine so she could listen again, but neither of them heard anything further.

"I'm probably losing my mind, but I swore I heard singing."

He paused for several seconds and then chuckled. "Yeah, I think it's all in your head. Maybe crazy runs in your family."

She gave his arm a friendly punch. "Take me home, officer, before I complain about being held without hearing my Miranda rights."

"Yes, ma'am."

Lucas deposited her at her doorstep a good ten minutes later, and she watched as he drove away. The sound of his engine faded into silence, and she turned toward the front porch. She'd come home at last, but things were nothing like she'd expected.

Interestingly, she was okay with that.

Dear Reader:

Thanks for joining me on the journey to Opal's world. I hope you enjoyed the story. If you did, please consider leaving a review. It's simple.

Return to the purchasing page.

Scroll down to the Customer Review Section.

Look for Review This Product

Click on Write A Customer Review

Your review helps me tremendously. It can be as simple as a short and sweet, "I liked it".

Also, make sure to sign up for my newsletter and/or follow me on Amazon for news of Book Two, BREWS AND BLOODSTONE, in the Crystal Cove Cozy Mystery Series.

Newsletter signup: www.CindyStark.com

Amazon: https://www.amazon.com/Cindy-Stark/e/B008FT394W

Thank you very much, and happy reading,
Cindy

Book List

CRYSTAL COVE COZY MYSTERIES (PG–Rated Fun):
Murder and Moonstones
Brews and Bloodstone
Curses and Carnelian
Killer Kyanite
Rumors and Rose Quartz
Hexes and Hematite

TEAS & TEMPTATIONS COZY MYSTERIES (PG–Rated Fun):
Once Wicked
Twice Hexed
Three Times Charmed
Four Warned
The Fifth Curse
It's All Sixes
Spellbound Seven
Elemental Eight
Nefarious Nine

BLACKWATER CANYON RANCH (Western Sexy Romance):
Caleb
Oliver
Justin
Piper
Jesse

ASPEN SERIES (Small Town Sexy Romance):
Wounded (Prequel)
Relentless
Lawless
Cowboys and Angels
Come Back To Me
Surrender
Reckless
Tempted
Crazy One More Time
I'm With You
Breathless

PINECONE VALLEY (Small Town Sexy Romance):
Love Me Again
Love Me Always

RETRIBUTION NOVELS (Sexy Romantic Suspense):
Branded
Hunted
Banished
Hijacked
Betrayed

ARGENT SPRINGS (Small Town Sexy Romance):
Whispers
Secrets

OTHER TITLES:
Moonlight and Margaritas
Sweet Vengeance

About the Author

Award-winning author Cindy Stark lives with her family and three sweet kitties in a small town shadowed by the Rocky Mountains. She dreams of moving to the Oregon Coast and splitting her time between walking the beach and penning more stories.

She writes fun, witch cozy mysteries, emotional romantic suspense, and sexy contemporary romance. She loves to hear from readers!

Connect with her online at:
http://www.CindyStark.com
http://facebook.com/CindyStark19
https://www.amazon.com/Cindy-Stark/e/B008FT394W